BENJI
THE WYLDE STREET BOYS SERIES
BOOK 1

N.R. WALKER

COPYRIGHT

Cover Artist: Pretty in Ink Designs
Editor: Boho Editing
Publisher: BlueHeart Press
Benji © 2025 N.R. Walker
The Wylde Street Boys Series © 2025 N.R. Walker

ALL RIGHTS RESERVED:

This literary work may not be reproduced or transmitted in whole or in part in any form or by any means, including electronic or photographic reproduction, except in the case of brief quotations included in critical articles and reviews, without express written permission.

This literary work may not be reproduced or transmitted in whole or in part in any form or by any means, including information storage and retrieval systems, or for use in AI training software.

This is a work of fiction, and any resemblance to living or deceased persons, companies, events or places is purely coincidental. Licensed images are used for illustrative purposes only.

TRADEMARKS

All trademarks are the property of their respective owners.

BLURB

Nolan O'Brien is a public prosecutor, and if he ever sees the name Bruno Barbieri again, it will be too soon. After a long week preparing for the trial of the decade, it takes no convincing to hit the men's club for a few drinks.

Except the club wasn't the only thing he hit that night.

Benji Smith works on Wylde Street as a rent boy. When he's chased by two men, he runs into the path of a moving car. With a no-cops, no-hospital policy and needing to escape the men following him, he agrees to go back to the driver's place.

The last thing Nolan expects is to offer Benji a place to stay, to recuperate, and to lie low. And the last thing Benji expects is to be attracted to the man who saved him.

But their worlds are about to collide in a way neither of them was prepared for, and both men need to decide what's at stake, what they're prepared to lose, and what they'll fight for.

benji
book one

N.R. WALKER

ONE
NOLAN O'BRIEN

"OKAY, O'BRIEN, PEN DOWN," Dominic said from my door.

I looked up in surprise, having lost track of the time. A quick glance at the city from my office window showed it was now dark. The office behind Dominic was quiet and empty.

"Shit," I mumbled, slinging my glasses across my desk and pressing my finger and thumb into my eyeballs. "Didn't realise the time."

"You also didn't realise it was Friday night and that you've had your head in that case file and completely missed lunch."

The twinge in my empty stomach agreed.

Dominic gestured to me and my desk. "So close your laptop. Put the files away. It's Friday night. Whisky and wings at 180, my friend." Then he clapped his hands. "Now, now, now."

I rolled my eyes at him as I stood up, plucked my suit

jacket from the back of my chair, threw everything into my messenger bag, and followed him out. I had to admit, it sounded good.

Dominic Lowing was forty-six years old. Exactly ten years older than me, and he was my senior at work. But from the minute we met, the day I'd started at the Office of Director of Public Prosecution's office, we just clicked. Maybe it was because we were the only two openly gay men at the firm. Maybe it was because we both worked long hours and understood how the game of law needed to be played.

Though I'm sure it was because we were both also members of the 180 club above Wylde Street, just around the corner from Oxford Street. An exclusive—meaning expensive—club for gay men. It was similar to a jazz bar—dark interior, mood lighting. It wasn't a place for cruising. There were no backrooms or bathroom blowjobs. There was plenty of that down on Oxford Street, if that was what you wanted. The 180 club was purely a professional men's club, where we could sit and talk business with a whisky in our hand.

Usually, after a few said whiskies and having solved the problems of the world, *then* we sought out the cruising options on street level.

Or found a backroom or a shady bathroom blowjob.

It was all I ever really had time for, and it suited me just fine.

Dominic and I stepped into the elevator. It was empty, so I thumped the button to the basement. "If I hear or see the name Barbieri one more time today," I murmured. Then I let my head fall back and I groaned. "Whisky sounds really good right about now."

Dominic chuckled. "It's almost over," he said. "And when Barbieri is behind bars for a really long time, there'll be another case just like his. And another, and another."

I barely resisted sighing. "Remind me why I do this?"

"Because you love it, and you're good at it."

Being on the prosecutor's team for the state government, getting to watch the Supreme Court in action, had always been my dream. It was now my reality, and while, yes, I did love it, my career meant zero time for anything else.

"You know what you need tonight?" Dominic asked as we walked to my car.

I threw my briefcase in behind the driver's seat and grinned at him over the roof of my Audi A5 Coupe. "I know exactly what I need."

He laughed because it was something else we had in common. The need for a few drinks on a Friday night at 180 and a tight arse to fuck my stress away.

Dominic was exactly the same.

Traffic wasn't too bad, and I found a park all too easily near Wylde Street, just off Oxford, as if the gods of terribly long weeks were finally on my side.

And as we walked to the door of 180, three young guys a few metres down the street caught my eye. One in particular, with curly black hair, tight black jeans, and a loose green T-shirt. He was a rent boy for sure, and he stopped and looked me up and down, licking his lips and making my dick stir.

Oh, I bet his mouth was good.

"Maybe a quick fix first," I said, and Dominic laughed as he grabbed my shoulders and led me to the entry.

"Wings and whisky first," he said. "A pretty boy to fuck later."

I protested weakly as we showed our IDs and Dominic shoved me into the elevator, and two minutes later, I had my first whisky in hand.

And then a second, and then a third.

We got talking with Leon and Marek, also lawyers, who had been in a committed relationship for twenty years. Nice guys, kinda quiet, and most people mistook their confidence for arrogance. It wasn't superiority or conceit. They were just so well-loved and well-understood by each other, there was a sense of power and complete trust that was hard to deny.

It was hard for me to describe because I'd never experienced anything close to that. But I looked at them with envy.

They were also incredibly wealthy, and it was almost impossible to not look powerful wearing $15,000 suits.

I ordered some wings and mini tacos, and I probably had a few of each, but the whisky was hitting differently tonight.

Because I hadn't eaten anything since a slice of toast on the way out the door at six o'clock this morning.

Then somehow it was almost midnight, and Dominic, Leon and Marek, and I decided to call it a night. Dominic wanted to see what the scene on Oxford Street looked like, but I just wanted to go home.

"Come on," Dominic tried as we hit the street. "You'll forget how tired you are once you find a pretty little thing to play with."

I looked down the street to where the three guys had been before, but they were long gone now.

Oh well.

"Nah." I waved him off. "Had enough. Going home. If I still want some arse when I get there, I'll order some. They have apps for home deliveries now."

Dominic laughed. "Fine. Suit yourself. Call for a lift," he warned. "Get your car in the morning."

Ugh. My car.

I'd forgotten.

"Evening, gentlemen," Leon said. "We're more in the mood for ordering in tonight as well."

Marek slipped his arm through Leon's and gave us a mock salute. "Next week, then," he said as they disappeared.

Dominic gave me a hard clap on the shoulder. "Be good."

"You be careful," I said, and he grinned as he turned and walked toward the crowded bars and thumping music.

I shook my head. How was he ten years older than me when I was the one going home early?

I considered calling out and following him, but all those whiskies I'd had were starting to circle the drain. I pulled my phone out of my pocket, fully intending to call a lift, but I also pulled out my car keys . . .

And my car was just right there.

And my apartment wasn't far. Barely a five-minute drive.

And I wasn't *that* drunk.

I was just tired. And I hadn't eaten enough.

So, making one of the stupidest decisions I'd ever made, I convinced myself I should drive home.

I got in behind the wheel, put my seatbelt on, and started the engine.

I pulled out onto Flinders, turning right onto Oxford, got into the left lane, and turned left onto Darlinghurst Road. Five minutes from home. It was too easy, and I was a good driver.

It'll be fine.

Everything will be fine.

Except I only got as far as Green Park when someone ran out across the road. I hit the brakes, but not before I hit them.

Holy shit. I just hit someone.

Scrambling and shaking, I got out of my car to find a guy lying on the road. He had curly black hair and black jeans, a green T-shirt. He rolled onto his side and blood ran down the side of his face as he tried to push himself up.

"Holy shit," I said. "Are you okay?" I went to him, putting my hands on him. "Stay still. I need to call an ambulance."

Dark and fearful eyes met mine. "No! No ambulance! No ambulance, please..."

The panic in his eyes, the fear; it frightened me. "But—"

"No hospital. Please. Need to leave. Before they find me. Please, please."

Then he slumped back to the road, his fist still clutching my jacket.

So, panicked, and before any onlookers could intervene, I did the second stupidest thing I could ever do.

I put him in my car and took him back to my place.

TWO
BENJI SMITH

I WOKE UP FEELING ACHY, stiff, and sore all over. Not the first time, either. But as I cracked my eyelids open, expecting to see the light in my dingy room, I realised I had no idea where I was. Or what time it was, or how I got here.

Wherever *here* was.

The room was big and dark. Expensive.

Dread snapped me awake and I jolted up, pain slicing through me.

"Stay there," a smooth voice said. "You're okay."

A man was kneeling in front of me then. Sandy hair, soft hazel eyes. Mid-thirties, at a guess. Stubble, strong jaw, concerned, exhausted. He looked somewhat familiar, but then again, a lot of faces looked familiar to me. He put his hand to my shoulder, barely touching me before he pulled it back, unsure if he should touch me.

"How are you feeling?"

I squinted my eyes shut, trying to remember . . .

Seeing two familiar faces on the street, certain they'd seen me. Certain they'd catch me . . . I remember running . . . I remember car headlights . . .

Shit.

I took stock of my body. I was still fully dressed—no sex, then—with a blanket pulled up to my waist.

"Where am I?"

"You're at my place," he said. "In Potts Point. My name is Nolan. You ran out in front of my car. I hit you . . ." His eyes flinched. "You have some cuts and scrapes. You asked me not to take you to hospital. I'm so sorry. Do you have pain anywhere?"

I tried to think. "Uh. Kinda."

The truth was, I did hurt. I hurt everywhere. From being strung too tight, always looking over my shoulder. From sleeping with one eye open for two years.

"I'm fine." I tried to get up again, but my body protested. As did Nolan.

"Please stay still. You're welcome to rest some more," he said. Then he gestured to the coffee table where there was a glass of water and a sleeve of pills. "I have some ibuprofen, but I didn't know if you have any allergies, or . . . and I thought maybe you should eat something before you take anything. Would you like some toast? I can make some toast. And coffee? Juice?"

Toast, coffee, and juice.

Mm, food.

My stomach wouldn't let me say no. These last few

years hadn't been easy, and I'd learned early on to let go of my pride and accept any offer of food.

"Uh, sure."

He smiled, changing his whole face. The concern was gone for a moment, replaced by a light in his eyes, and there was the hint of a dimple.

I was always a sucker for a dimple . . .

He disappeared behind the couch, and I could hear him in the kitchen. A plate on a countertop, the toaster being pressed down, the fridge door opening and closing. Then I heard coffee beans being ground.

Real coffee?

I sat up slowly, taking in the room. Open plan, expensive furniture. My shoes were placed neatly by the couch, my phone screen down on the coffee table.

I checked my pockets for my key to the apartment, thankful when I found it.

I turned then to watch Nolan. He wore a long-sleeve Henley and some jeans that probably cost more than my rent. His kitchen was the fancy kind, and yeah, it was one of those expensive coffee machines with its own grinder.

I could smell it.

I'd grown up with all these riches, and god, how I'd missed good coffee.

Nolan turned, coffee cup in hand, and he smiled again when he saw that I was sitting up. "Here," he said, bringing me the coffee. "Do you take sugar?"

"No, thanks," I replied. I used to take sugar but hadn't had the luxury in a long time. I was used to going without.

I sipped it and sighed at the taste.

My forehead felt tight, and a quick touch to my hairline found a Band-Aid. Oh.

Then I remembered . . . when I'd seen those men last night, I'd ducked so fast to hide that I'd cracked my head on the lid of a dumpster.

And then I'd ran . . . Across the unlit park and onto the street . . .

Fuck.

A second later, Nolan was back with a plate and a glass of orange juice. "Just plain butter," he said with a grimace. "I wasn't sure if you liked peanut butter or Vegemite."

Oh my god.

Hot toast with butter . . .

I tried not to shovel it in. I tried to act like it was no big deal, but the way he was watching me, it was impossible not to be embarrassed.

"Sorry," I mumbled, sipping the juice.

The juice was even better than the toast or coffee. Cold, fresh, and so good. The expensive kind. I remembered taking this shit for granted.

I could feel Nolan staring at me, so I avoided making eye contact. I knew how I looked—like I hadn't eaten in days.

"I'll make you some more," he said, taking my plate and glass. When I handed the glass over, I caught his eye. I expected to see pity or loathing, but no. He was smiling. "Plain toast okay again? Or would you like peanut butter?"

I was never saying no to peanut butter.

"Uh, sure, that'd be great, thanks."

He went back to the kitchen. "Take some ibuprofen," he said. "You've got some scrapes; it will help with any aches."

I snatched up the sleeve of pills, popping two and downing them with the coffee.

It was then I noticed another blanket on the single-seater, as if he'd slept there to keep an eye on me.

Probably to make sure I didn't steal anything.

"You had a cut on your head," he said. "I cleaned it up last night with some antiseptic and put a Band-Aid over it. It didn't look too deep, thankfully. Do you have a headache?"

I did have a scrape on my elbow. Road rash by the look of it. And my side felt all tight, probably from where I'd hit the asphalt. I had no rips in my jeans, thank fuck. But my knee was sore, and my back. And my head.

"I'm okay," I replied. I snatched up my phone. "What time is it?"

My phone said it was 7:43 am, and I had a lot of messages from Fitch.

"Oh, I kept the blinds drawn," Nolan said, bringing me over more toast and juice. "I wasn't sure if your headache would appreciate the morning sun."

Peanut butter . . . oh, it was heaven.

The crunchy kind too. My favourite. After one big, mostly respectable bite, and tasting how fucking good it was, I shoved the whole slice into my mouth. "Need to check in," I said with zero manners, as I quickly thumbed out a reply.

> I'm okay

"Check in with whom?" Nolan asked cautiously. "I can drive you anywhere you need to go. You're not stuck here or my prisoner or anything." He cringed again. "I just wanted to make sure you were okay. You said no hospitals, which I can respect. Though you should know, in your line of work, you have rights and are due full respect and are entitled to free medical care—" He grimaced again. "Sorry."

Well, I hadn't expected all that. Especially the part about rights and respect.

"My line of work?"

He baulked. "Uh, yes. I've seen you working on Oxford Street," he said quickly, putting his hand up. "If I'm wrong, I apologise. I don't mean to offend or assume."

He looked so horrified I couldn't help but smile. "I'm not offended, and you're not wrong. Well, we work Wylde Street, technically, not Oxford. It's our spot," I said. I wasn't offering any explanation on the no-hospital thing. Instead, I showed him my phone screen. "I check in with my friends. We have a rule. We check in with each other. It's a safety thing."

He was clearly relieved. "Oh, that's good. And smart."

But then my phone vibrated with a call. It was Fitch

and we rarely ever called each other, so I answered it straight away. "Hey."

"Benji, thank fuck," he said. "Where are you?"

"I um, I'm in Potts Point. Where are you?"

"At home. Look, I'm coming to you. Pin me your location." It sounded as if he was walking, and he sounded panicked.

"What's wrong?"

"He's looking for you again. Those two men were asking questions."

I scrubbed a hand over my face, hitting the Band-Aid on my forehead, making me wince. "Yeah. I saw them," I admitted quietly.

"Did they see you?"

"I . . . I don't know. I ran, but I got hit by a car—"

"You what?!"

He screeched that so loudly, I had to pull the phone away from my ear, and I noticed Nolan cringe. Not at the noise. More at the getting-hit-by-a-car part.

"I'm fine," I said to both of them. "I slept on his couch, and he just fed me breakfast."

"I can drive you wherever you need to go," Nolan said quietly.

"He said he can drive me," I repeated to Fitch.

"No. You need to not be seen. I'm coming to you. We'll figure something out. Send me your location."

The line went dead.

I checked my screen, and yeah, he'd hung up. I sighed. "He doesn't take no for an answer," I explained. "He's coming to get me. I can meet him out front."

His eyebrows furrowed a fraction. "Is he . . . are you safe with him? If he doesn't take no for an answer, then—"

I laughed. "No, he's my best friend, well, one of them. He's just the bossy one."

I went to Maps and pinged my location to him.

Nolan seemed to school his face; his expression neutral. "I uh, I didn't mean to overhear, but he said someone is looking for you?"

My stomach dropped and tightened all at once. "It's nothing. It's just . . . It's no big deal."

"If you're not safe," he said gently, "I can help you."

"Help me?" He had no idea.

"I can get you help. There are services available for people in situations such as yours—"

I put my hand up. "No, thank you. It's fine. I don't need any services." The truth was, I couldn't use them. I couldn't use my real name. "Thanks anyway."

He frowned at that and sighed. "Look, I feel terrible about what happened. I'd been drinking and I shouldn't have driven. I know better, and it was stupid and irresponsible. And dangerous. You could have been seriously injured. Are you sure you're okay? Would you like a hot shower before you leave? Is there anything I can get you?"

He'd been drinking? I hadn't known that. Not that it made any difference.

"Pretty sure I was the one who ran out in front of your car," I said. "Thank you for not involving the cops."

He barked out a laugh. "Uh, I should be thanking

you." He squinted his eyes shut and shook his head. "Jesus Christ. This is so bad."

He seemed to be taking this so much harder than me.

"We're all good," I said. "No harm, no foul."

But then I stood up and my back twinged. I couldn't stop the wince. And I had to pick up my shoes, so I bent slowly. Yeah, this wasn't good.

It was just a twinge. An ache. My hand went to my back, and I bit back a groan.

Nolan was quick to grab me. "Okay, you're not fine. Lie back down. Take some more ibuprofen. Maybe after a hot shower, you'll feel better. I have some heat rub too. That might help." He helped me lay back down and he took my phone. "I'm going to tell your friend to come up."

He texted his apartment number to Fitch and showed me the screen before he put the phone on my chest.

"I feel so bad," he mumbled.

"It's just a strain," I mumbled. "I'm sure I'll be fine in a bit."

But yeah, that hot shower sounded really freaking good.

He sat on the coffee table, watching me. And I dunno why, but his worry for me was nice. He was a decent guy, and that was a rare trait to find.

"So," I said, trying to lighten the mood, "you've seen me on Oxford Street, huh?" Then I remembered something else. A super gorgeous man in a suit heading into 180 . . . Hmm. That's where I'd seen him. Just last night. It seemed fitting, given how exclusive that place was and how expensive his apartment was. He'd been interested, but his friend had led him inside.

We were lucky that our spot on Wylde Street was close to 180. It meant higher paying customers. Didn't always mean we'd get treated any better, but the money was good.

"No, not Oxford. Wylde Street, huh? You go to 180."

He nodded slowly. "I saw you last night," he said quietly.

I liked that he admitted that.

"Right. Before, you know, you hit me with your car." His face was a horror show, and it made me laugh. "Sorry. Still too soon?"

"Yes. I think it will forever be too soon for that to be funny."

"So, was it a nice car at least?" I smirked at him. "Because if I'm going to get hit by anything, can it at least be a nice car?"

He almost smiled. "Still too soon for jokes."

Then something occurred to me. "Shit. Is your car damaged? I can't pay for that—"

He shook his head and again went to reach for me but stopped himself. "No damage. And the car isn't important. I'm more worried about you. Is your back feeling any better?" Then his eyes lit up. "Oh, I have a heat pack. Let me go find it for you."

He disappeared, muttering something about where he'd last seen it, and I found myself smiling. Despite everything that had happened last night, despite the twinge in my lower back. Nolan was a sweet guy.

He came back out carrying a wheat pillow. "Found it. I had a hamstring injury a few years back," he said. He put it in the microwave just as something else chimed. "Oh," he said, going to a monitor by the door. I hadn't noticed it before. "Hello?" he asked.

A familiar voice replied. "I'm here for Benji."

"Ah, Benji," Nolan said, glancing my way. I realised then that I hadn't given him a name.

"That's Fitch," I replied. "You can let him in."

Nolan buzzed him through, and I considered sitting up again but my back said no. A few moments later, Nolan opened his door and Fitch stepped in.

"Hi," Fitch said. Then he saw me and rushed in and sat on the sofa with me, his hand on my arm. "Jesus, Benji, are you okay? What the fuck happened?"

"I'm fine. I've just strained my back. It'll be right in a few hours."

Or a day or two.

He put a gentle hand on my hair. "And your head. You got hit by a car? What the fuck?"

"'Twas my fault," I said quietly. "I saw—" I glanced at where Nolan was in the kitchen, not wanting to say too much. I lowered my voice anyway. "Those guys, and I hit my head on a dumpster, of all things. Then I took off through the park and ran into the path of a moving car."

Nolan came back then with the heated wheat pack. "Here," he said quietly. "Lean against the sofa with this pressed against your back. Where does it hurt?"

I tried to reach around to show him, realising too late that arm had the scraped elbow. "Down low."

"Please, allow me," Nolan murmured. He placed the wheat pack against my lumbar area and gently leaned me back so the sofa would keep the pack in place. The relief was almost immediate. Then he pulled up the blanket. "Can I get you anything else?"

I don't know why, but his kindness touched me. I was sure I blushed. "I'm fine."

Fitch looked between us, questioning, smiling, and far too obvious.

"I'll give you guys some privacy," Nolan said, fidgeting, unsure, before he turned and walked down a hall.

Fitch's eyes met mine. "What the fuck was that?"

I chuckled. "He's a nice guy. He feels bad."

"Considering he hit you with his car, he probably should." Then he double-checked that Nolan was gone. "Did you fuck? Because he's hot."

"No," I said. "Considering, you know, he hit me with his car." Then I sighed. "How the hell am I supposed to work tonight? I already missed making money last night."

"Benji, that's the least of your worries. You-know-who was looking for you last night. Those two guys must have seen you because they spent the rest of the night searching up and down Oxford for you. You can't work the street. You shouldn't even go back there, not for a few days at least."

"The fuck am I supposed to do? Not even about working, Fitch. But I live there."

"We'll have to get you inside. I should have brought a hoodie with me. I'll go back and get it. Then you'll just have to hole up for a few days. Give your back some time to right itself."

I groaned. Our apartment was dry at least and better than sleeping rough, but it was a shithole. No TV, no anything. "It's just a muscle strain. Fitch, I need to work," I said. "Or I won't even have the shithole apartment."

"Me and Ky will cover rent for you—"

"No. I can't ask you to do that," I said. We barely had enough money for food as it was. "I'll just . . ." I shrugged. "Hit Grindr or something."

"You know how shady that gets."

"What choice do I have?"

"You can stay here," Nolan said.

Fitch and I both turned to see him standing near the hall. "I didn't mean to eavesdrop," he said. But then he walked over and stood by the coffee table. He seemed genuinely torn. "But it's my fault you're injured, and I feel bad. Stay here. Just for a week."

Fitch and I both stared at him. I was shocked, but Fitch smiled slowly. "That's perfect," he said.

"I can't," I mumbled. "Thank you for the offer." Then I stared at Fitch, so he'd understand. "I need to work."

"I'll pay you," Nolan said, his brow furrowed.

He'll what? Pay me?

What the fuck?

"Pay me for what?"

"I mean, I'll cover your rent," he corrected. He fidgeted a little and grimaced. "I didn't mean it to sound as if I meant anything untoward."

Fitch snorted. "Untoward? Who the hell uses words like untoward?"

I nudged Fitch with my knee to get him to quit being an arse when Nolan was being so nice.

"He'll do it," Fitch said. "Thank you, Nolan, is it?"

He gave a nod. "Nolan O'Brien."

Wait, what? "I never said yes," I tried. The offer was tempting, and over-generous. And offers like that never came without strings.

"Benji," Fitch said seriously, patting my arm. "You need to hide out for a week, this place is a fucking palace, and he'll cover your rent. You're a hooker, he's rich. What part of the Pretty Woman fairy tale don't you get?" Then he looked Nolan up and down. "If he says no, I'll stay for a week. You can cover my rent and do whatever you want to me."

I nudged him again. "Fuck off, Fitch." Then I sighed because as much as I didn't like it, Fitch was right. "Fine. I'll stay. If it will make you feel better."

"It will," Fitch replied.

"I wasn't talking to you."

Nolan's eyes met mine. "If it will make *me* feel better?"

"Yeah. You said you feel guilty."

"I do."

"I ran out in front of your car," I said.

Nolan shrugged one shoulder. "But still . . ."

Fitch clapped his hands together. "Then it's settled. Benji, you're staying here. For a week—" He looked around the room. "—in this luxury apartment with the hot-as-fuck rich guy. And he's gonna cover your rent. Tell me, Nolan. Wanna run me over too? How do I get in on this gig?"

Nolan surprised me by chuckling, that dimple pressing into his cheek. "I'd rather not."

But Fitch was right, again. Maybe a week here in this luxury apartment with the hot-as-fuck rich guy wouldn't be so bad. He was even gonna cover my rent. If it made him feel less guilty, then I wasn't gonna say no.

THREE
NOLAN

THE OFFER for Benji was out of my mouth before I had time to stop it. He couldn't work, which was my fault, and to think he could lose his apartment? Covering his weeks' rent, from what I gathered by his shithole-apartment comment and the fact it sounded as if he shared with Fitch and someone called Ky, couldn't have been more than a hundred bucks. Maybe two. I'd spent more than that on a bottle of whisky...

The fact he was hiding from someone was probably something I should have delved into a little deeper before offering him to stay at my place. But I could only imagine the kinds of thugs on the streets who tried to squeeze money or favours out of sex workers...

Or drugs.

Oh shit.

"Uh," I said. "Just some ground rules though. I should have said this first. No drugs, no clients, nothing illegal, and you don't share my address with anyone. Not that

I'm assuming or judging, because I'm not, I just need to be clear that I can't be involved in anything illegal."

"Like hitting people with your car?" Fitch said with a cheeky smile. He was a funny guy, apparently. But Benji gave him a knee. "Just kidding," Fitch added. "Benji here doesn't do drugs or even drink much, really. That's why the three of us stick together. Me, Benji, and Ky. We don't touch that shit. And if he is unable to work this week, with the no-client rule, then can he expect remuneration for loss of income?"

"Fitch," Benji hissed at him.

"I'm bargaining on your behalf," Fitch hissed right back at him.

Why did I like this guy? Fitch was good looking. He had floppy brown hair and a cheeky grin that I was sure worked well in his favour in his profession.

But he was charming, and he clearly cared about Benji. And he said that he and Benji and Ky—I assumed made up the three guys I'd seen on Wylde Street last night—didn't touch drugs.

And I had to admire Fitch's tenacity.

"Financial remuneration, huh?" I said to Fitch. "How much does one earn in a week?"

"Six hundred," Fitch said.

Benji baulked and tried to knee him again, but his back twinged.

Six hundred bucks. I had no idea if that was even close. From Benji's reaction, I was guessing no. It was more than generous. But what was the alternative?

Them reporting me to the police for a hit and run?

How many thousands would that cost me? What was my reputation worth? My career?

"Six hundred total, inclusive of rent," I replied.

"Deal." Fitch grinned.

Benji's expression was more concerned, maybe even offended?

"Cheer up, buttercup," Fitch said. "You're welcome, by the way. Now, I'll go grab you a bag from home. Need anything in particular?"

Benji opened his mouth and closed it again. "I dunno," he whispered. He rattled off a few items but was still stunned by my offer, I thought. Or maybe he was in pain.

And a fresh wave of guilt washed over me. "Benji, how about you go and take a steaming hot shower? Stay in there for a while, let the hot water work its magic on your back. I'll drive Fitch back to grab your bag. And I'll run past the supermarket for whatever you need."

Fitch brightened. "I'll come to the supermarket with you and grab him everything he needs."

"Fitch, stop," Benji said softly.

Fitch ignored him completely. "Come on, little injured lamb, let's get you up and into the shower."

Fitch helped him up and I showed them the way to the bathroom, then left them to it. I changed into some jeans, then realised Benji might need some clean clothes. His clothes would need a good soak . . . or an incinerator. But I found him some sweatpants and a shirt that would all probably be a mile too big on him, but if he was resting all day, at least he'd be warm and comfortable.

I heard them having a somewhat heated whispered conversation in the bathroom before I knocked. "Uh, I just have some clean clothes," I said.

The door opened and a smiling Fitch appeared. "Thank you." He put them on the vanity, and I could see a now-shirtless Benji in the bathroom. He looked a little too thin and there was some red rash on the back and side of his ribs. Where he'd hit the road last night, by the looks of it.

I felt so much worse.

"Okay," Fitch said. "Benj, you have as much hot water as you need here, I'm guessing."

I nodded.

"Take as long as you need," Fitch said to him, softer this time. "I'll be in touch, pretty much non-stop, so you won't have a chance to miss me."

Benji snorted.

"And if the sexy, rich guy tries anything, you must call me," Fitch added. Then he looked me up and down again. "Because I wanna watch."

Benji shoved him out of the bathroom and closed the door. Fitch looked up at me. "Ready when you are."

I wasn't sure how ready I was to go shopping with Fitch. "Ready as I'll ever be," I said.

It was hard not to like him. He was easygoing, charming, had a grin that was made of mischief, and he was also a very loyal friend to Benji.

He had the knack to talk, leading conversations without giving anything away. In the supermarket, he had no problem throwing things into my basket. "Benji likes these," he'd say, throwing in random items. Fruit and vegetables, cupcakes, and even a phone charger.

I didn't even mind.

But I'd seen the way Benji had sighed and closed his eyes when he'd sipped the juice, so I grabbed some more of that. And some more bread and peanut butter.

Then I drove to Oxford Street, nabbed a park, and Fitch raced down the street. I didn't see which apartment complex or alley he went into, but he was back just a few minutes later with an old backpack, grinning as he climbed into my car.

"All good?" I asked.

He gave me that grin. "Yep. I'll come back and check on him one last time," he said. "Before the no-visitor rule comes into effect."

Figuring there was no point arguing, I began the drive back to my place. "It was a no-client rule. So unless you're a client, it doesn't apply to you."

He laughed. "Hell no, I'm not a client. Not that I'd have to pay him, but I'm not inclined to deliver what he needs, if you get my drift."

I did not, and apparently my face said as much.

"He needs a top," Fitch explained. "And while I will partake if a john pays me to, I'd much rather let them do the work. Get what I'm saying?"

I nodded, feeling foolish. "I get it now, thanks."

Fitch laughed. "Lucky you fit that bill. I mean, I assume." He looked me up and down again. "You do top, right?"

My face burned, letting him know he assumed

correctly, but I wasn't saying it out loud. But then I thought about what he said. "What do you mean lucky I fit that bill? I'm not paying him for sex. That's not . . . that's not what I'm paying for. I'm paying him because it's my fault he can't work."

Fitch chuckled. "Let me tell you something about our Benji. He has needs. Sexual needs. But I'll let you two discuss that."

I stared at him between glances at the road. "What? What do you mean we'll discuss that?"

He sighed and waved a hand, apparently ending that line of questioning. "I do appreciate you offering him a place to lie low though."

This conversation was . . . a lot.

"Can I ask who he needs to lie low from?"

"Well, you can ask," he said with a sigh. "It's just thugs on the street. We deal with them a lot. People trying to take our spot, that we're too close to their corner, that kind of shit."

Hm.

I wasn't sure I totally believed that, but I really had no clue about the politics on territory for sex workers. Maybe there was truth in it.

"All you need to know is that it's not drug related because we don't do that shit. We're rent boys, not mules or users." He shrugged. "Our world is hard enough without that shit."

I dropped it then because he was right.

Their world *was* hard enough, and I had no clue about the actual reality they lived every day.

As I pulled into the underground parking of my very nice apartment complex, amidst the other expensive cars, it was very apparent that I lived in a different world than these boys.

"You don't seem to have any problem with us being rent boys though," Fitch said as I shut off the engine.

"Why would I?"

"Most people do," he said simply. "They look down at us, or worse, just pretend we don't even exist. But not you."

"I see all people," I said with a shrug. "As people. I don't know the first thing about how or why people end up where they end up, and that's not for me to judge."

God, if my job taught me anything, it was that.

"Everyone's just trying to get by, doing what they have to do," I added, which felt contrite, given it was much easier to 'get by' in an expensive car and luxury apartment than it was for Fitch and Benji. "I value human beings and their right to be treated with respect."

Fitch snorted and rolled his eyes. "Jesus, you're a Disney prince." He took the backpack and got out of my car. "Remember my offer. You want to hit me with your car anytime, my offer stands."

Good lord.

"I'd rather not, but thanks."

He went to the front of the car while I grabbed the groceries. "There's not even a bump or a dent. Are you sure you hit him?"

I looked around, grateful we were alone. "Yes," I hissed at him. "But it was more of a bump and him falling back. If I'd hit him hard, he'd have broken legs and a head wound."

"True." Fitch slung the backpack over his shoulder and took a bag of groceries from me. "Anyway, let's go see how my favourite boy is."

"Favourite, huh?"

"One of them. Ky's my other favourite. He was still asleep when I went back home. As long as I know we're all safe, I'm good."

I hit the elevator button. "The three of you stick together, huh?"

"Always."

That was all he said until we walked into my apartment. Benji was lying on the sofa, cleaned up, his washed hair in damp curls, and wearing my clothes.

He looked brand new.

He sat up with a wince, and Fitch threw his backpack to him. "Grabbed you a few things. You'll have to let me know if you need anything else and I'll bring it over during the week."

I had to stop myself from saying I could buy him whatever he needed. I wasn't entirely sure why I was offering as much as I was, but they had so little—dirty clothes, worn shoes, a stained backpack—and I had more than enough to help them.

They fell into a quiet conversation and I unpacked the groceries, bringing over the few non-food things Fitch had thrown into the basket. Deodorant, toothpaste, soap, razors, a pack of underwear, and some socks, plus the phone charger. It was all stuff he'd take home with him in a week's time, but that was okay too.

I made two sandwiches, packed with ham and salad, and set them on the coffee table before them. I could guess that Fitch probably hadn't eaten in a while from the way he inhaled his sandwich.

"Well, I should get going," Fitch said eventually. "I have things to do before work tonight."

"Check in with me," Benji said. "No matter what time. Just let me know you're okay. And Ky too. I'm still around if you need."

"I know," Fitch said. "Just keep a low profile."

Benji nodded. "I will."

"Oh," Fitch said, opening the backpack and dumping the contents onto the sofa between them. "I got your essentials. Everything you'll need for a week."

There were a few things: a notebook, his old broken-looking phone charger, some old hand-held game console, three boxes of condoms, lube, and a box of PrEP.

Oh, dear god.

"Jesus," Benji said, shoving them back into the backpack. "Essentials my arse."

"Exactly. Essentials for your arse. I know you, Benj. You'll be climbing the walls soon. And Nolan's a top. I already scoped him out for you."

Benji looked at him, horrified, and I barely managed to put my hand out in a defensive manner, shaking my head, but before I could speak, Fitch kissed Benji's hair. "Oh, that shampoo smells so good. Goddammit, sure you don't want to swap places with me?"

Then, before anyone could say anything else, Fitch laughed, waved a cheery hand at us, and was gone.

Benji sighed. "I'm sorry about all that."

I tried to appear unruffled. "It's fine. I like him. He has a certain . . . charm."

Benji looked at me and chuckled through another sigh. "He does, yes. The kind of charm you can't help but like, as much as you try not to."

That made me smile. "He's a very good friend."

"He is." Benji met my eyes. "Thank you, for everything. For what you bought for me. Or, I should say, what Fitch made you buy for me."

"Think nothing of it," I said. "Are you feeling better after your shower?"

He nodded. "Much. My back is still a little sore. It's just a twinge though. Muscular, that's all. It'll be fine in a day or so."

Not if he slept on the couch . . .

"Uh, this is . . ." I cringed. "This is going to sound bad, please don't misunderstand. But you should probably sleep in my bed." His gaze cut to mine, so I quickly added, "There's a TV in there, you'll be more comfortable. The mattress is one of those Posturepedic ones. It'll be better than the couch."

"This couch is a hundred times better than my bed," he replied.

"And I've slept on that couch more times than I'd like to admit. It's fine," I allowed. "But if your back is sore, the bed is better. I can take the couch for a night or two. I didn't mean to imply anything."

He laughed. "I didn't think you were implying anything."

"Well, the offer is there," I said, then realised how that sounded. "For the bed, not the offer for implying anything . . ." I shook my head. "God, I'm sorry."

He laughed again, his whole face lighting up. He looked younger and carefree when he laughed, when his dark eyes lit up, shining like his beautiful black curls.

I had to wonder how he'd got to this point in his life. What led him to be a rent boy, as Fitch had called themselves. I doubted it would be a happy story and that made me sad for him.

This bright and beautiful boy should be living his best life, not as a sex worker and hiding away in a stranger's apartment for safety reasons.

And given he was staying with me for a week, I figured some general conversation and basic information wouldn't go astray.

"So," I began. "How old are you, Benji?"

"Twenty-one."

"I'm thirty-six," I volunteered.

"And you said you can't be involved in anything illegal," Benji said. "This place is far too nice for you to be a cop, so I'm going with something professional. And you did tend to my cut, and you seem more concerned about my well-being than most, so maybe something medical?"

I snorted. "No. I'm a lawyer."

"Ah. Makes sense. Your apartment, your nice car. Do you get to say 'you can't handle the truth' and shit like that?"

"Well, I'm legal counsel. I mostly do groundwork for the people who get to say that."

He nodded slowly. He didn't say outright that he didn't like lawyers, but he didn't have to. "Right."

"My name's Nolan O'Brien, by the way," I offered, hoping it would prompt him to give me his surname. It didn't. "And your last name?"

He seemed surprised. "Oh. Smith. Benji Smith. Original, huh?"

Smith.

It absolutely was not his name.

"Nice to meet you, Benji Smith."

He gave me a fake smile and picked up the TV remote. "So, what should we watch?"

FOUR
BENJI

I DON'T KNOW why it was so hard to lie to him.

Maybe because he'd been so generous, so kind. And that was a rarity in our world. It usually came with conditions and was a transactional exchange.

Men were usually only nice to me to get what they wanted from me.

But I wasn't lying to him to deceive him. I was telling him the not-truth to protect him. The only person who knew my real name was Fitch.

Ky knew I had a not-so-nice history, but there wasn't one person in our profession that didn't. We all had issues: abuse, abandonment, desperation.

People rarely went into sex work willingly. It was because of limited options and no other choice.

Did I have other options? Any other choice?

Maybe.

The only choice I had was either escape, selling my body to keep my heart and soul free, or stay in my old life and have it cost me more of my soul than I was prepared to give.

And anyway, I found Fitch and Ky, and the three of us were as tight as brothers. We promised we'd keep each other safe, keep each other out of trouble and away from the dark path of drugs and bad shit.

We were our own family, and that was our life preserver. We didn't need drugs when our escape from reality was the bond between us.

I understood why many of our other friends did though. To escape the pain and misery the only way they knew how. The only way they could.

It was a crying shame and evil of those who preyed upon them.

I had no time at all for those arseholes or anyone who would use the vulnerability of others for personal gain.

Like my father.

"Have you had enough to eat?" Nolan asked.

I'd zoned out, staring blankly at the TV and not seeing or hearing a word of the movie I'd picked.

"Oh yeah, thanks," I said. "I haven't eaten this much in ages."

Admittedly, I'd only had breakfast and a sandwich for lunch, but still, two meals a day was more than enough these days. I didn't want to spoil myself and have my stomach used to regular feeds because next week, I'd be back to my old life of maybe a cup of cheap ramen a day.

"How's your back? Can I get you anything?"

"I'm okay," I replied. "My back's feeling better already. But I might get up and walk around for a bit."

He shot up from his seat and offered his hand. "Here, let me help you."

I almost laughed, because I wasn't that injured. "It's fine, honestly."

Having someone fuss over me felt really good, but it also felt wrong. I kept waiting for him to state the terms of his generosity, to tell me what he expected in return, but he didn't. He was just . . . nice.

I got to my feet, slowly but unassisted and without wincing. "See?"

He was standing a little closer and had his hands out as if he wanted to touch me but wasn't game. "Are you sure?"

I stretched my back a little. "Yep. You don't need to fuss."

I met his eyes then. Hazel, soft.

Kind.

Damn, he really was sexy. He had that intelligent and confident demeanour that I found incredibly attractive. There was no superiority, no conceit. It was a fine line to tread, but he did it well.

And his kindness. The biggest turn-on for me.

Nolan was ticking every box I had but I didn't want to ruin his very generous offer by crossing lines. If I was going to be staying here a week, I needed to be on my very best behaviour.

"I'm just gonna do some laps of your hall, if that's

okay?" I asked, thinking some distance between us was for the best. "I think I need to move or I'll seize right up."

"Oh, sure, of course," he said, moving out of my way. "And remember, the offer to use my bed still stands. If you need to lie flat, or whatever . . ." He did that cute grimace thing again. "You had some grazes on your back as well. If you need me to apply some antiseptic cream, I can. I saw them when you were in the bathroom, sorry. I didn't mean to see, but you were shirtless, so . . ."

"Ah, it's just a bit of gravel rash," I said. I stretched my arm up to prove that it wasn't anything to worry about. "Nothing too bad."

He seemed somewhat convinced. "Okay." He gestured to the messenger bag on the table. "I'm going to get some work done."

"Will my walking up and down the hallway disturb you?"

He pulled out a laptop. "Not at all."

I did a few laps while he typed away. I couldn't see the screen from where I was, not that I'd have looked anyway. He was focused on his work, like I wasn't even there, so I did a few more laps and then a few more.

It wasn't far, down the short hall, across the living space to the front door and back again, but it did help with my back. My legs needed the stretch, and so did my mind.

I wasn't used to sitting around and resting. The last two years had been a wild ride, every day was something new. Our apartment was small and there wasn't anything in it to keep us occupied. No books, no television. So we never stayed inside. There was always something happening on the street. Oxford Street was a hub of activity, day or night.

The park, the cafés, the shops were our social meeting place. And we didn't only work at night. Daytime trade was a thing. Businessmen on a lonely lunch break, delivery men at any time of day, regulars who needed a quick BJ after a meeting...

The thing was, and this was something not many people understood, I enjoyed my work.

For the most part anyway. There were always exceptions, of course. But I was a sexual person. I loved dick. And since I'd come out at eighteen and began living my truest life, I hadn't gone two days without some kind of sex.

I enjoyed the social aspect of living on Oxford Street and working the men who cruised there. It wasn't a perfect life, don't get me wrong. I didn't want to be a sex worker growing up, but this was the situation I'd found myself in, and I had to make the best of it.

Except now I'd found myself spending a week in a lavish apartment with a hot, older rich guy. Which was great and all, and I appreciated the safety of his place. It was exceptionally generous and kind of him.

But how was I supposed to spend a week here without any social interaction? Without sex?

After my twentieth lap of his apartment, after I'd sat back down and tried to watch some TV while he typed away, I decided more laps were in order. Nolan looked engrossed in whatever he was doing, but with each step, I was getting more bored and more antsy.

And, if I was being honest, it kinda bugged me that Nolan could ignore me walking back and forth. But he intrigued me, and in the end, it got the best of me.

Now, normally I avoided all personal questions, but one thing in particular begged to be asked.

"So, Nolan," I began. I waited for him to look up from his laptop screen. "Any boyfriend or partner who might take issue with me being here?"

He clearly wasn't expecting me to ask that. He blinked in surprise. "Ah, no." He shook his head. "None. Work keeps me busy enough."

I pulled out a seat at the end of the dining table. "Do you cruise Oxford Street often?"

He closed his laptop and smirked. "Not really, no. When the need arises."

When he needed sex, that was.

"You go to that exclusive club? The 180 on Wylde?"

His eyes met mine, holding my gaze. "Yes."

"I saw you go in last night," I admitted.

He grinned, keeping eye contact. "I saw you too."

"I thought you might have been interested before your friend led you inside."

He barked out a laugh, his cheeks pinking a little. "I, uh, I don't recall."

I snorted. "Is that a lawyer defence line?"

He smirked as he ran his thumb across the lip of his laptop. "I'm not at liberty to say."

That made me laugh. "So, big bad lawyer, huh?" I

looked pointedly around his living room. "You must be good at it."

He looked up at me then. "I am."

Hm. Confident. I liked that. "So, what do you do for fun?"

He drew a deep breath in and sighed on the exhale. "Fun . . . I don't really do anything for fun. I go to the gym, though that feels like a chore most days. I stopped playing cricket when I tore my hamstring."

"Fair enough." I nodded slowly. "Do you read? Go to the movies?" I shrugged. "Trying to think of what normal people do for fun. I'm not too familiar."

"Normal people?"

"Yeah, people like you."

"I'm not sure if normal is appropriate for anyone as it implies someone who is abnormal."

I snorted out a laugh. "Sorry. Forgot I was dealing with a lawyer."

He smiled. "What about you? What do you do for fun?"

"Well, we don't have a sex worker's cricket team, if that's what you're wondering."

He chuckled. "You should start one. No reason why you can't."

I counted off my fingers. "Registration fees, uniforms, sporting goods."

He winced. "Sorry."

"It's fine. Can't say cricket would be my first choice anyway, so it's really fine."

"Do you have any other hobbies?"

I thought about the things I used to do, that I missed from my old life. At first, I used to miss the luxury things like my game consoles and my car, but after a few years, it really was the simple things I missed the most. "I used to read when I was young. Loved King and Koontz but haven't had the luxury in a while."

"Do you like to read?" He seemed surprised by this. "I have plenty of books. All kinds. In my bedroom."

I raised an eyebrow. "You seem very keen to lure me into your bedroom. First the offer of your bed, now your books..."

He rolled his eyes and stood up. "Come with me." I stood up and he went to grab my elbow but stopped himself. "Is your back okay?"

"Yeah, it's feeling better already," I said. "Walking helped."

He nodded. "Good." Then he gestured back to the hall. "Come this way."

I followed him to the door on the left of the hall. He opened it and walked into what I could now see was a large bedroom. The bed itself was expertly made, the covers a dark grey, the wall behind it black, the other walls were grey, and black curtains hid what appeared to be a decent-sized window. There were black accents, black furnishings, and along the wall opposite the bed was a TV mounted on the wall and a low bookcase underneath it, the entire length of the wall.

"Wow," I breathed. "Nice room."

He cleared his throat. "Thanks. I like it."

If I was a gazillionaire, I'd have my room exactly like

this. As it was right now, I was lucky to have a mattress on the floor.

And the books and the huge TV were amazing, but the bed . . . Damn, it looked comfortable. Big and pillowy soft, and I was pretty sure if I ever slept in it, I'd never want to leave. "I might change my mind about taking your bed instead of the couch. How do you make yourself get up every morning?"

He chuckled. "Some days it's not easy." Then he swallowed. "The offer still stands, by the way. Your back really would do better if you slept in here rather than on the couch."

My back wasn't an issue, but I was considering saying yes anyway.

Then he waved at the bookcase. "And books. You can choose whichever you want. They're mostly alphabetised. Fiction, non-fiction. Whatever you like. You're here for a week, so read away."

I looked back at the bed and imagined myself sitting up against the headboard, reading. Living it up like a king. Part of me didn't want to overstep, but wow, part of me—that sounded a lot like Fitch—was telling me to live up every single thing I could while I had the chance.

Nolan laughed. "You want to try the bed, don't you?"

"I do," I whispered. "But I don't want to make it weird."

Chuckling, he gestured to the side closest to the window. "Go on, try it."

Go on, do it now while you have the chance Fitch's voice said in my head.

I went to the far side and sat down, sinking into the softness, the wealth of it.

I slowly laid down, my head on the pillow, and sank into the pillowy heaven...

"Oh my god," I breathed.

Nolan chuckled as he walked over. "Nice?"

"Oh god, I've missed this," I replied. I didn't really mean to say that out loud. I'd done a pretty good job at convincing myself I missed none of my old life. I learned early on that it was a dark path to go down and one that only led to heartache, and I'd done a good job of avoiding it. But maybe remembering the books and the bookcases at my parents' house earlier had opened a door I'd long thought closed.

But my old bed, in my parents' house, had been big and soft like this. Soft fabrics that weren't scratchy. A mattress built for back support and not just the cheapest one available.

This was expensive, as it had been in my parents' house...

"You should rest in here," Nolan said, walking over to the other side of the bed. For a second I thought he was about to lie down on his side, but he didn't. "At least during the day. Sharing a bed at night could be a little weird." He made a face and tossed the remote control onto the bed beside me. "Not weird because it's you, exactly. I'm just not used to sharing a bed with anyone, and I don't really know you, that's all."

Then he mumbled something to himself and shook his head. "Watch some TV if you like," he said, nodding to the remote he'd thrown over. "Or grab a book. Whatever you want. I'll be out at the table. We'll have to think about dinner soon, I guess. I'm not sure what you feel like, so have a think and let me know . . ."

He cringed again, clearly awkward, and I hated that for him.

"I'm not used to it either," I said as he got to the door. "Sharing a bed with anyone. For what it's worth. I've never done that."

I felt stupid for saying that.

He stared at me from the doorway. "You've never . . ."

I snorted. "I know what you're thinking. Yes, I've done many things with men, but sleep next to one?" I shook my head. "Never."

A smile pulled at the corner of his lips before he gave me a nod and disappeared down the hall.

I considered turning the TV on but decided against it. The silence was perfect for imagining I was floating on a cloud. My blinks were getting longer, the lure of sleep edging closer with every deep breath.

There was no outside noise, no traffic, no yelling.

I was safe here.

I was showered, in clean clothes, with a full belly, and on the most comfortable bed ever.

Sleep hit me like a truck.

I WOKE up to the smell of something delicious,

something spicy and sweet, and my stomach growled. I followed the scent, seeing it was getting dark outside.

Nolan was stirring something on the stove.

"Smells good," I said.

He startled. "Oh, hey. I hope you like curry."

"Love it." The truth was, I loved any food that wasn't home-brand ramen. "I didn't actually mean to fall asleep, but damn, that bed . . ."

Nolan chuckled. "You must have needed it."

"Did you get your work done?"

"I did." He nodded. "Well, as much as I could get done today."

"Isn't today Sunday?"

"It is."

"You work on weekends too?"

"When it needs doing. I actually get more done at home than in the office. And it gives me a head start on Mondays."

I looked around his kitchen. "Need me to do anything?"

"Uh . . . Can you set the table? Placemats are in the cabinet behind the table."

"Sure." I liked that he asked me to do something. It made me feel useful, and it only took opening a few drawers to find what I needed. I set the table with him at the closest end and me at his right. I didn't want to sit opposite him, as far as body language was concerned. I wanted to have conversations with him, not interviews. I poured us a glass of water each and he soon put two bowls of rice and curry on the placemats.

"This smells so good," I said, waiting for him to sit first. I slid into my seat, almost salivating at the rich aroma. "I haven't had a proper home-cooked meal in so long."

He smiled so easily. "Well, I hope you like it." He nodded to the bowl. "Dig in. There's plenty more too."

I took a small mouthful and sighed when the flavours exploded on my tongue. I even did a little wiggle in my seat, and Nolan laughed. "Oh my god," I said. "You made this?"

"I don't cook often," he said with a nod. "Kinda got used to it just being me and can't be bothered. It's easier to pick something up on the way home or get it delivered. Less mess too."

I ate a few spoonfuls of rice, sauce, vegetables, and chicken, savouring every burst of flavour. I had to try and remember my manners so I didn't shovel it in like a heathen.

"You don't cook?" he asked between bites.

I shrugged. "Not really. Our kitchen is tiny. The stove top works but the oven doesn't. I eat more ramen than could ever be good for me."

"Your landlord should fix your oven," he said. "You have rights as tenants."

That made me chuckle. "You see the world through the lens of a lawyer. It's cute."

"Cute?" He laughed. "Never been called cute before."

He was ridiculously handsome, a little grey at his temples, and he got those creases at his eyes when he laughed. It struck me hard that I found him so attractive.

And that this was the closest thing to a date I'd ever had.

"So is this what dating is like?" I asked, only then realising how that sounded when his eyes cut to mine. "No," I amended quickly. "I know this isn't a date but is this what it's like? Dinner at some guy's house, talking and laughing as you eat home-cooked food."

He smiled as he chewed and swallowed. "I guess. Have you never been on a date before?"

I shook my head. "Nope. Kinda cut the niceties and formalities and skip straight to the happy ending, if you know what I mean."

He nodded, still smiling. "Well, there's something to be said about that method too."

"What kind of thing?" I didn't mean to sound so defensive.

"That it's valid," he replied smoothly. "Some people don't have the time or means for the niceties and formalities, as you put it. They have needs to be met, like everyone, without the preamble of dating. So yes, it's a valid means to an end."

I thought about that and expected him to find sex work denigrating or beneath him, but he didn't. At least I didn't think so.

"Especially with the likes of Grindr these days," he added. "There's barely any need for preamble at all."

"You use apps?"

He shrugged. "I have. But I don't like the

anonymity of it. Most guys I know love it for that very reason, but it feels impersonal to me. Which is, again, why most men I know love it." He sighed and sipped his water. "I'd prefer to meet someone face to face and have a conversation before we get to the happy ending part."

This surprised me. "You are not in the majority."

Of course, he laughed. "Oh, believe me, I know. And I've done the nameless, faceless fucks before. In nightclubs, backrooms, glory holes." He shrugged. "I'm past that scene now. I'd rather have dinner with someone and have actual conversations before we get to the fucking."

I chuckled and put my hand to my heart. "Such a romantic."

He laughed again before he ate some more, and I really loved that we could talk so freely about sex.

"Most clients I have need the anonymity, and apps can be traced and tracked," I explained. "Those guys don't want names or conversations, and that's fine. Then I have some guys who just want companionship. Most times sex, but not always. They're just lonely."

He nodded slowly, frowning. "I'm glad you help them."

"Some guys have hang-ups and weird kinks that their partners wouldn't understand."

He smirked at me. "I bet you have some stories."

I laughed as I nodded. "Oh yeah." I paused for a few seconds. "Not that I can divulge anything."

He laughed at that. "Not that I'd expect you to."

We ate in silence for a while. It wasn't awkward at

all. Quite the opposite, actually. I was comfortable with him, and it took me a few moments to figure out why.

"You don't seem bothered by my line of work," I said.

He met my gaze, clearly surprised. "Why would I be?"

I shrugged. "Most people are. Some are appalled. At best, some just pretend they don't know. They certainly don't talk and laugh about it."

His eyebrows drew together. "I'm sorry if anyone made you feel lesser than you deserve. I don't see it as a bad thing. Certainly not something to be appalled about." He chewed on his bottom lip for a second. "In fact, I'm kind of fascinated by it. Not in a weird, fetishising way."

I snorted.

"I just . . ." He sighed. "Some people can't get past the stigma, and that's on them, not on you. It's no different to any other paid work, and at the end of the day, like most other jobs, it's just what you do. It's not who you are."

I stared at him, stunned. It was rare that I was rendered speechless. I'd learned how to school my reactions, keeping emotions bottled away. I could go with the flow 99% of the time. No matter what a john said, I could act as if I'd expected nothing less.

But this genuinely surprised me.

Because being a rent boy was just what I did. It wasn't what defined me. And to hear him say that, for him to believe that, made my chest all tight.

"What about you? Is being a lawyer what you do or who you are?"

He smirked at me again. "I'm probably fifty-fifty. I uphold the law, and I'm a law-abiding citizen. But what I do is mostly just paperwork, making sure legal cases are watertight; *i*'s dotted and *t*'s crossed. That kind of thing. I'd like to think I'd be remembered for more than my job."

Damn, if I wasn't smiling at him. Not an act, not to get what I wanted, not to appease the paying customer.

"I like you," I said. "You're a *good* person."

He seemed a little offended. "Oh, thanks."

"Believe me when I say that's a freaking rarity in my world. Being a good person, doing the right thing when no one's watching is like winning the lotto."

He chuckled quietly. "Well, I guess being called a good person is better than being called *nice*."

"But you're nice too."

He put his hand to his heart, pretending to be hurt. "Ow. I'm wounded."

I laughed. "And you're sexy as fuck. And rich! And you're very generous and kind, and an awesome cook. Believe me, you are like winning the lottery, and the fact you're single is a crime."

He grinned at me. "A crime, huh?"

"Yes! A crime. There should be a line of men at your door. The fact there isn't makes me wonder . . . do you have some insane fetish I don't know about?" I looked around his apartment. "There's no locked door with a hazmat sign on it or a chest freezer full of body parts, right?"

He stared at me.

I stared right back. "Right?"

Then he barked out a laugh. "No! I'm law-abiding, remember?" He chuckled. "Jesus. What kind of shit have you seen?"

I laughed with him but pretended to zip my mouth and throw away the key. "No can tell."

He put his hands up. "Good. I don't want to know. That way I can't be incriminated."

I sighed and collected our plates. "Let me clean up," I said, but when I stood, my back twinged again.

Nolan was quick to grab my arm. "You're not okay," he murmured. "I'll take care of these. You go back to bed. I'll bring you in some more pills and the heat pack."

He took the plates from me and set them back on the table. He was standing close enough for me to feel the warmth of his body, and with his hand still on my arm, he proceeded to lead me back to his bed.

I could have protested, but damn, if it didn't feel good to be looked after . . .

By him. This kind and genuine person. It didn't hurt that he was hot and that his apartment was like a five-star hotel, but he was gentle and caring.

So I let him lead me to his room, to his bed, and he fixed the bedding, sat me down, and once I'd got myself situated, he pulled the covers up.

God, I could get used to this.

I didn't dare to get used to this.

I could enjoy it while I was here. It had been so freaking long since I'd had anyone tend to me, care for me. Sure, Fitch and Ky looked out for me, as I did for them, but they'd never tended to me.

Not like Nolan did.

"I'll be right back," he said. "Do you need anything else?"

"My phone," I replied. "Sorry to be a pain."

"It's no bother," he said with a smile before he disappeared out the door.

He came back with a glass of water, a sleeve of pills, and my phone. "It's still only ibuprofen. I might duck down to the chemist and see if I can get something stronger over the counter. And some muscle rub."

"You don't have to do that," I tried.

"It's no problem." Then he cocked his ear. "Oh, that's the microwave. Hang on." He was gone and came back a moment later with the heat pack. "Okay, try this."

He helped me sit up, pressed the heat pack to my lower back, then gently laid me back down. It felt so good that I didn't have the heart to tell him the pain wasn't that bad.

I didn't mean to play it up, but my god, he was so attentive.

So attractive.

He popped two pills and helped me sip the water to get them down. And all I could do was take in the line of his jaw, the column of his neck, the concern in his eyes, how his tongue swiped across his bottom lip.

"Everything okay?" he asked.

I laughed quietly. "Never better."

"I mean your back."

"It's honestly not that bad. I just stood up wrong."

He frowned at that. "Hm. I could call a doctor—"

"No," I said, trying to sit up, but with his hand on my shoulder, he urged me to stay still.

"Okay, no doctor," he relented. "But I'll get some more pills and some heat rub. I won't be long. Any requests?"

"If I said you didn't need to do that, would you listen?"

He considered that for half a second. "Nope."

I rolled my eyes but kinda laughed. "Fine."

"I'll be ten minutes."

I lay there in the dark and quiet, absorbing this new feeling of being looked after. It was a warm and fuzzy sensation, with a good dose of longing and an edge of sadness and grief.

Longing to have this forever, sadness to know that I couldn't, and grief for the last time I felt cared for was when I was a kid.

Before my mother left, and before my father was free to be the arsehole he is . . .

Nope. Don't go down that path . . .

I picked up my phone and saw I had a few messages from Ky, asking how I was and if I needed anything. And from Fitch.

> So, tasted his dick yet?

Then three minutes later . . .

> Is that why you're not replying?

> Are you too busy getting railed right now? I bet he has a great cock

I snorted in the quiet room.
And another two minutes later . . .

> Okay you're gonna need to reply or I'm coming back to check on you

I thumbed out a quick reply.

> Calm down. I'm fine. Not getting railed though and no, I haven't tasted his dick yet. We were having dinner.

His text bubble appeared immediately.

> Dinner? As in actual food and not his dick?

> LOL yes. Then my back was sore so he put me in his bed where I am right now

I knew what he'd reply to that and I wasn't disappointed.

> You're in his bed right now and you're not being railed? WHO ARE YOU AND WHAT HAVE YOU DONE WITH BENJI

> LOL aren't you supposed to be working?

> I am

> How's business?

> The usual. Ky's busy with the two daddies

I smiled at my phone, knowing how much Ky liked those two men. They were an established older couple who liked a young thing to play with. They treated him well and paid him double. He was always happy when they texted him for a play date.

> Good for him

> Gotta go. Duty calls

> Be safe. Text me when you get home

There was no answer forthcoming, and I knew he'd have pocketed his phone to give a prospective client his full attention.

I scrolled my socials for a bit, finding nothing of interest. Until I decided to search up the name Nolan O'Brien.

I found professional stuff, like LinkedIn and some corporate photos of him in expensive suits and million-dollar smiles, but there was nothing else.

I guessed as a lawyer he knew better than to plaster personal information online. If he had a Grindr profile, he didn't use his real name, which wasn't surprising. Very few did.

Like I could talk.

Then before I could forget, I sent Fitch another text.

> Hey forgot to tell you I told Nolan my surname is Smith, Benji Smith, jsyk.

I didn't wait for a reply. I put my phone on the bedside and decided to try the TV instead. I was still scrolling Netflix when I heard Nolan come home.

The front door opened and closed, then the sound of keys on the kitchen counter and quiet footsteps before he appeared at the door with a bag in his hand.

"Hey," I said, putting the remote control down.

"I wasn't sure if you'd still be awake."

"Yeah, my little nap earlier fixed me right up. I'll be awake for half the night now."

He came in and walked to my side of the bed. "How's your back?"

I resisted sighing at his over-concern and decided to allow myself this one luxury. "It's really not so bad."

Nolan sat on the edge of the mattress, near my hip, and he reached into the bag and pulled out a bottle of Sprite. "Thought you might like one of these."

Oh man.

"Hell yes," I said, slowly sitting up.

Nolan took my arm and helped me. "You okay?"

I nodded, taking the bottle. "I haven't had real Sprite in so long. If I get anything, it's just the cheap home-brand stuff. Which is fine, but it's not the real thing." I cracked the lid and took a quick sip. "Ah, it's spicy."

He chuckled. "Spicy, huh?"

"Proper Sprite is spicy. Trust me."

Smiling, he took a tube from the bag. "I also got some of this," he said. It was some heat rub for muscles. "And some more salve for the grazes on your back. If you lift your shirt, I can put it on for you."

Oh.

"Ah, sure," I said quietly. I tightened the lid on my Sprite and set it next to my phone, then pulled my shirt up to expose my back.

Nolan moved up and, with the gentlest touch, he applied the salve first. "It doesn't look deep or anything," he murmured, his voice soft and deep.

And I was all too aware of how close he was, how his touch was more of a caress, how his voice felt like a velvet brush over my bare skin.

Fitch's words echoed in my mind.

Tasted his dick yet?

You better be getting railed . . .

My body was hyperaware of him now. His warmth, his size. God, how I liked a man with a decent build.

"How does that feel?" he whispered.

I turned my head in his direction, half looking over my shoulder, playing into the whole damsel-in-distress thing. If he wanted to care for me, and I wanted to revel in it, then why not?

"Much better," I purred. "You have great hands."

His hand stilled, his breath caught, and it was a full few seconds before he pulled his hand away. "Now for the heat rub," he said, not whispering this time.

Did he not want to play this game?

He applied some cream to his hand, and I could smell

the liniment immediately. It reminded me of locker rooms and half-naked footballers . . . and now my body was on board.

"Love that smell," I murmured.

"Hmm," he said. "Whereabouts on your back?"

I reached around to my lower back. "Just here."

He began rubbing it in. Harder this time, really rubbing it in, and oh boy . . . yeah, I was not going to last a week here without having sex.

Some kind, any kind of sex.

He was working the heat rub into my lower back in firm circles, and my god it felt so good. All of it. His touch, his body close to mine, the scent of liniment. I couldn't stop the moan that escaped me. "God, that feels good."

I heard him swallow hard and his hand slowed to a stop. Then he cleared his throat and pulled my shirt back down. "There you go, all done," he said, standing up.

Pretty sure he had a bulge in his pants, but he collected the bag, holding it in front of himself, and headed toward his bathroom. "Need to wash my hands," he said as he disappeared.

Damn.

Yeah, okay, so that sure was something.

I lay back down, my back feeling much better, and my dick hard. And I was sure of one thing. This week of staying with Nolan, if he wasn't going to rail me, was going to kill me. Either that or I had to do my best to convince him to fuck me.

He was paying me, after all.

He really should get his money's worth.

FIVE
NOLAN

I SHUT the door to the bathroom and leaned my back against it, trying to catch my breath.

Jesus Christ.

I needed to jerk off or something. It wasn't right that I was having such a physical reaction to Benji. He was exactly my type, yes. Gorgeous, with younger, boyish charms. Was a twenty-one-year-old too young?

Yes.

No.

Yes . . . No. God fucking dammit.

He was an adult. He was very familiar with sex, and he knew exactly what he was doing when he moaned like that and looked at me over his shoulder with those fuck-me eyes.

Christ.

But he was here because he needed to recuperate and hide out for a week. He was injured. I was looking after him, not preying on him.

Or was he preying on me?

That sound he made . . . damn. It sparked fire in my bones.

I had to remind myself that he was a sex worker. A rent boy. He knew exactly what sounds to make, how to play it up. How to play me.

Did he think I expected sex?

Was that what that act was?

Maybe I hadn't been clear enough from the beginning.

I didn't expect anything like that . . .

Except now I couldn't stop thinking about it. What other sounds he'd make, what he'd feel like when I buried myself inside him, him underneath me, riding me.

No.

I shot off from the door, going to the sink and washing the heat rub off my hands. Cold water and fragrant soap were a good distraction from the sultry scent of a gym locker room rendezvous.

I splashed some cold water on my face and looked myself dead in the eye in my reflection.

"Act your age," I mumbled sternly to myself. "Show some restraint."

Hm. Yes, restraint.

I shook out my shoulders, letting the tension slip away, and I urged my dick to behave, then went straight to the kitchen to clean up after dinner.

It was another good distraction, as was the work I did on my laptop for two hours. Benji hadn't stirred or come out of my room, and while I understood he was there because I'd told him he could lie in my bed, I hadn't exactly meant that he could spend the night there.

I'd assumed he'd come out at some point and settle on the couch again, but he hadn't. When I went in to check on him, he was on his side facing me, sound asleep. The room was dark, the only light coming from the hall, casting a soft strip of colour across his features.

He was pretty. Beautiful, even.

Pale skin, a few freckles, long eyelashes, and full lips. His dark, curly hair topped off his boyish features.

It was easy to see why he used the term rent boy.

Young, thin, cute.

I considered waking him but figured he could use the sleep. It wasn't like he was wide awake and eagerly patting the bed for me to join him . . . Then I considered taking the couch as I'd said I could . . . as I probably should. But the selfish part of me wanted to sleep next to him. It was a huge bed and I could stick to my side of the bed and not disturb him . . .

My god he was so beautiful.

He was asleep, and I was being a perv for watching him without his knowing.

So I got myself ready for bed, dressed in pyjamas—sleep pants and a tee—and slid into bed as quietly and gently as I could.

He didn't stir.

I was almost disappointed.

Okay, so I was disappointed.

And annoyed at myself for being so.

I was dreading going to work in the morning, possibly

for the first time ever. I didn't want to leave Benji here by himself. Not that I feared he'd skip out on me, taking whatever he could sell with him.

I didn't think that at all.

I didn't want to go to work tomorrow because I'd enjoyed his company so much. I hadn't had someone over at my place for any length of time, and the company had been amazing.

Having someone to talk to, to laugh with, to eat with.

I got the feeling he wouldn't be staying for the whole week, and I was going to miss having the company. Which was a stark reminder of how lonely I was.

How reclusive I'd become, and how much of my life centred around my work.

With a weighted sigh, I rolled onto my side with my back to him and closed my eyes.

I WOKE up too warm and far too comfortable, and as I came to grips with my surroundings, I realised why.

Benji was using my arm as a pillow, curled into my side, his head on my chest.

What the fuck?

I had no recollection of moving, and a quick assessment of how I was in the middle of the bed told me that we'd both moved toward each other.

I'd opened my arm for him at some point and he'd snuggled in.

I didn't want to move. I didn't want to wake him, and I didn't want to go to work today.

I wanted to stay with him. I wanted to do a lot of things to him, but that wasn't going to happen. He wasn't here for my pleasure; he was here to recuperate and stay out of trouble for a week.

Trouble I probably should have asked about but didn't want to know . . .

With him lying in my bed with my arm around him, I wasn't sure I cared.

My god, how I wanted this . . .

I wanted intimacy, human touch, and the feel of a warm body next to mine.

I wanted sex.

My dick was very aware of Benji's proximity.

Goddammit.

I need to get up and out of bed now.

My alarm hadn't even gone off, but I needed to be out of this bed before he woke up and realised I had a raging hard-on.

"Morning," he said, still half-asleep. I froze, but he chuckled. "I probably should apologise for being where I am right now." He sighed. "But I'm not sorry. Like, at all. That was the best sleep I've ever had."

I realised belatedly that I still had my hand on his shoulder. I let it drop. "I should get up," I said, pulling my arm free and sitting up, swinging my legs to the floor.

Willing my hard-on to miraculously deflate.

No such luck.

Benji whined out a sigh. "Such a shame."

I had my back to him and didn't dare turn around to see, but it definitely sounded as if he were pouting.

Don't look. If you see those lips in a pout with sad dark eyes, you'll do something you'll regret.

"I need to shower," I said quietly and walked into my bathroom so he couldn't see just how much I'd enjoyed having him in my arms.

I made the shower as cold as I could stand, and it did very little to rid myself of my eager cock. Well, the hard-on was gone but the urge, the need for release was bubbling just under the surface.

You're not going to work today.

You're going to work from home. You've done it before, that time when you weren't feeling well, and it was fine. Working from home was common these days. It's no big deal . . .

I shut the water off and grabbed my towel, mad at myself for even entertaining the idea.

This is a one-off. How often do you have a guest staying over? Get your work done and enjoy his company. Life will be back to miserable and lonely soon enough.

Goddammit.

No, go to freaking work. Christ.

Now even madder at myself, I dried off and regretted not bringing clothes with me. Because now it meant that I had to walk back out into my room wearing nothing but a towel.

With Benji still in bed watching me.

Except he wasn't. The bed was empty, and I was both disappointed and grateful. I quickly pulled on my briefs and suit pants, getting dressed for work. I pulled on a work shirt, buttoning it up, convincing myself that work would be good for me.

I needed to be busy and buried in paperwork.

Except when I walked out to the kitchen, threading my belt on, Benji was standing at the counter, wearing pyjamas with bed hair, slicing up some fruit. "Coffee machine is on, and I thought I'd fix you some breakfast before you leave."

"I'm not going to work today," I said out loud, surprising even myself.

He paused, the knife mid-slice through a strawberry. "Oh?" Then he looked me up and down at how I was dressed. "Where are you going?"

"I'll work from home," I said. "I was going to go into the office, but honestly, I get more done at home, and you're here by yourself and I feel bad for leaving you. If I go into the office, I won't be home until late, and that's not fair."

He was stunned, almost as much as I was, by the words that came out of my mouth.

"I can watch TV and read a book," he said. "You don't need to miss work on my behalf."

I shook my head. "I'm not missing anything. I'll still need to get work done, and if I do need something from the office, I can have it couriered. It's not like I'm calling in sick or anything. I'll just sit at the table, and I have noise cancelling headphones, so the TV won't bother me. You can watch whatever you want."

He smirked as he finished slicing the strawberry. "So you still wear the suit to work from home?"

I looked down at myself and chuckled. "Ah, no. I'll go change."

He grinned at me. "Okay. Is fruit and coffee okay for breakfast? Some toast, maybe?"

Having him smile like that, all sleep rumpled in my kitchen, making me breakfast? He had no idea . . . "That's . . . Perfect."

I went back into my room and changed into some more comfortable clothes. Some new lounge pants and a long-sleeve tee shirt seemed more appropriate. I refused to look at myself in the mirror because I couldn't bring myself to look myself in the eye.

I was refusing to go into work because I had a sexy little rent boy as a house guest.

What had my life become?

I was never this irresponsible.

I never did shit like this.

Maybe that's why I needed to do it . . .

Life will be back to normal next week.

I took out my phone and sent a message to the office that I'd be working from home as I'd come down with a cold.

It wasn't a sick day, as such; I didn't need a medical certificate. I was just simply working from home. People did it often these days. I had no meetings, no appointments, so it was no big deal.

That's what I told myself, anyway.

I also sent Dominic a text.

> Working from home today. On email if needed. Call if it's urgent.

And then, because I'd already thrown all responsibility out the window, I switched my phone to silent.

I came back out to find two places set at the island counter, not at the table. Coffee, juice, toast, and sliced fruit.

"This looks great, thank you," I said.

He grinned, looking me up and down. "And you look much more comfortable. I had to look through a few cupboards to find everything. Hope that's okay."

"More than okay," I said, pulling out a stool to sit on.

"I didn't know what you wanted on your toast," he said. On his plate was one slice of toast cut in half with a smear of peanut butter.

I took half, grinning as I bit into it. "Peanut butter's fine."

"Hey!" He laughed, swatting at my hand.

But then he took my plate and spread some peanut butter on the toast, cut it in half, and stole one of my halves. His playful smile and sparkling eyes caught me by surprise, and I had to make myself look away. I sipped my coffee as a distraction.

"Did your friends check in after last night?" I asked.

"Yep. All is well." He nodded, popping a strawberry in his mouth. Which of course, made him groan. "Oh, that's so good."

I was still stuck on that filthy sound he just made.

"You like strawberries?" My voice was rougher than I'd intended.

"Mmm," he said, having another and making another obscene sound that curled low in my belly. "That's so good. I haven't had fresh strawberries in years." Then he did a cute little happy wiggle. "This is all so good. You're spoiling me so much I won't want to leave."

I found myself smiling at him, at how happy fresh food made him. I wanted to ask what his story was, how he came to be working like he did, but didn't want to ruin his mood.

We had a week to delve deeper into personal waters.

I wondered if he'd tell me. And I wondered how bad it might be, and then I realised maybe I shouldn't even ask. Maybe I should give him a week to escape from his reality.

"You'll have to think about what you want for dinner. We can order something if you'd rather I didn't cook."

He smiled behind his coffee. "Or I could cook," he suggested. "I haven't done that in a while and I can't promise it'll be any good, but it's the least I can do." He raised an eyebrow. "You're paying me, after all."

"I'm not paying you to cook though."

"We haven't really discussed what you're paying me for," he murmured. One of his eyebrows rose artfully, his smirk far too sultry.

"I'm covering your rent and loss of income because I hit you with my car," I replied. "I don't expect anything in return."

He sighed, then smiled as he sipped his coffee. "You

can put me to work if you want," he said, his eyes meeting mine. "I have . . . certain skills."

Jesus.

My body knew exactly what he was implying but my brain had to intervene. "Breakfast was great, thank you. Maybe you can work on some lunch-making skills around midday." I checked my watch as I stood up. "I should get busy."

Benji smiled, watching me as I stole a slice of strawberry and put my plate in the sink.

"I think I'll watch a movie," he announced. "Seeing as I have hours to fill in."

"Good idea."

"I can watch in your room, if that's okay. That way I won't distract you if you're working at the table."

"Of course. Though you can watch out here. I'm good at tuning out noise. I don't mind one bit."

He pouted as he considered this, and damn, if he didn't do it deliberately. Like he knew what those full, pouty lips did to me. "I might get lonely in your room," he murmured. "Your bed is too big for one person."

Yep. He knew exactly what he was doing.

I laughed and shook my head. "Does playing the sweet boy win over all your clients?"

He smiled, biting his bottom lip. "Yes."

"I can see why."

His eyes lit up and I swear he purred. "So you'll join me?"

I put my hands up and went to the dining table. I needed to put some distance between us, and it helped that he couldn't see my semi-hard dick that these stupid lounge pants did little to hide. "No. I have work to do."

He sighed petulantly and even stamped his foot, but then his phone rang. He answered it, looking right at me.

"Fitch, Nolan's being mean to me," he said.

I scoffed. What the fuck?

I heard Fitch say something, but Benji shook his head. "No, no. He's just being mean. He won't spend the day in bed with me."

I heard Fitch laugh, then he said something else.

"My back's fine . . . Yes, of course I tried pouting . . . And what? It didn't work . . . Nothing. He still said no."

Oh, dear god.

If only he knew how on edge my body was. How my balls ached and how my dick was only one more of Benji's pouts away from being a full hard-on.

Working from home had been a very bad idea.

"I'm going to watch a movie," Benji said. "*Pretty Woman*, because you know, real life imitating art and all that." Then he paused by the table and looked at me. "Though I'm sure Richard Gere's character railed the hooker he was paying to stay with him for a week."

Jesus. He was just saying this out loud?

He wasn't even hinting anymore.

He wanted me to rail him?

Benji sniffed and went to the couch where he picked up the remote and lay down as the TV came to life. No longer paying any attention to me, having a mumbled conversation with Fitch.

My mind was still stuck on what he'd said—on the

me-railing-him part—while my dick was very much on board, my eyes were having a blinking contest with the cursor on my laptop screen.

I couldn't believe what he'd said.

My phone screen came to life with a text from Dominic. It was a good distraction to kick my brain into gear. I picked up my phone, ignoring what Benji was saying.

Dominic's text was blunt and to the point, just like him.

> Everything okay?

I thumbed out a quick reply.

> Yeah. Just not feeling great.

Which was a lie . . . Or maybe it wasn't. I was feeling . . . some kind of way. Mostly confused, somewhat enamoured with the sassy guy on my couch with the full pouty lips who wanted me to rail him, and definitely aroused.

Yes, definitely aroused.

All while I wasn't feeling not great as I'd lied to Dominic, I was certainly feeling the most alive I'd felt in a long time.

The fun, the company, the excitement.

The prospect of giving Benji what he wanted . . .

This was not going to end well.

I slid my phone onto the table, put my headphones in,

and tried to block out the world as I busied myself with actual work. I had reports and data for depositions to do, and it was good to be productive.

Though I saw on the screen when Benji found *Pretty Woman* on Netflix, and I saw when Julia Roberts got in the car with Gere.

I looked up again when Benji, still lying on the sofa, raised both hands in the air. Julia Roberts was telling the store on Rodeo Drive of their big mistake, and it made me smile.

It was a great scene in the movie about not judging a person by their clothes or their job.

And Benji identified with Julia Roberts's character.

Both sex workers.

Both deserving of respect as human beings.

In some ways it reminded me of why I did what I did for a living too. To make sure people were treated fairly and justly the only way I knew how.

I went back to my work, almost done on this one report. But I looked up again in time to see Richard Gere climbing the fire escape to rescue his damsel.

I pretended to not notice when the movie ended and Benji walked past. I heard the shower start and I pretended to not envisage him wet in the shower.

He came back out and I pretended to not notice how low-slung those sweatpants were on his hips, how his hip bones peeked out below the hem of his too-short tee shirt. I most definitely didn't notice the outline of his dick or the way I was certain he wasn't wearing underwear.

I stared at my laptop screen so hard my eyes hurt,

though the words were a blur. My heart was hammering, my blood running warm.

My dick was in a permanent state of semi-hardness.

Then, of course, he stopped walking and turned back around. "Forgot my book," he murmured.

Which I was certain he did to make sure I'd look up at him and see him in those slutty clothes with his wet curls and sweet smile.

And yeah, he was most definitely not wearing underwear.

I let out a slow, quiet breath as soon as he'd disappeared, trying to get my body and mind back on track.

I deliberately didn't look at him when he walked back past with a book in his hand, and I didn't look at him when he lay back down on the couch.

I did smile as his foot appeared on the top of the backrest though . . . until I realised it meant he was lying there with his legs spread wide . . .

He was going to kill me, I was sure of it.

I decided checking emails was in order, and a decent distraction as it turned out. I hadn't thought of Benji for a few minutes, at least, until he appeared beside me with a plate in his hand.

"Your lunch," he said, sliding the plate toward me. There was a sandwich on it, and I hadn't even realised he'd gotten up or heard him in the kitchen.

"Oh, wow. Sorry, I lost track of time." I checked the time on my laptop. It was after midday. Jeez. I really had lost track of time.

"You were in the zone there for a while," Benji said. "Will you stop for lunch? Or do you work through?"

"Uh..." I half shrugged. "Normally I eat as I work. But I've never had a house guest before. I can take a few minutes."

He brightened, genuinely happy about this. "We can sit on the balcony!"

I chuckled at his enthusiasm. "Okay."

We took our plates out to the balcony, and man, the warm sun on my face, the fresh breeze, was a small slice of heaven I hadn't allowed myself in so long.

The sandwich was great too, and the way Benji was smiling.

He looked even prettier in the sunlight. It highlighted the shades of dark blues and gold in his black hair, and his freckles looked bronzed. His long eyelashes fanned shadows across his cheeks when he closed his eyes, soaking up the sunshine.

Boyish. Beautiful.

"I would never leave the balcony if I lived here," he murmured.

I sighed, the sun making me sleepy. "I forgot what it feels like to take a minute of sun for no other purpose than to feel it warm my skin."

He opened his eyes slowly, smiling at me. "You're so poetic."

I chuckled and stretched out. "Poetic? I was going to say if I was a cat I'd be purring right now."

That made him laugh, and when he stretched his legs out too, his foot brushed mine. He didn't move it away or apologise. He just sat there, smiling at me with our feet touching.

It felt oddly intimate.

A rush of butterflies flittered in my belly, and I was reminded of the first time I'd held a boy's hand in high school. That jittery rush . . .

God, I haven't felt that in so long . . .

"Are you getting through your work?" he asked quietly.

"I am."

"What time will you be working through till?"

"If I were at the office, it'd be six or seven."

"Damn."

"So maybe six?" I hedged. "Did you want to order something in for dinner?"

"No, I want to cook you something. I don't know what yet. I'll go through your pantry and fridge and see what I can come up with. I feel bad for not doing anything. I hate being lazy."

"You're not being lazy. You're resting. Is your back feeling better?"

"Much. You were right about your bed." His eyes held mine. "Great spinal support. I bet its real comfy to fuck in."

I very nearly sputtered but managed to rein it in. He chuckled at whatever my face did though. "You're so easy to rankle."

"Rankle?"

"Yes. It means to make someone annoyed."

"I know what it means. I'm not annoyed. I just find your blasé commentary about sex somewhat shocking."

"Shocking?"

"Yes, it means to cause a feeling of surprise or dismay."

He laughed and he tapped his foot to mine. "Ah. The man has wit."

I found myself smiling at him, and as much as I shouldn't have enjoyed this banter, I really freaking did. "The man needs to get back to work."

He sighed then, pouting with huge puppy-dog eyes. "Aww, but we were just getting to the good part."

Yes, we were.

Which is why I needed to stop it.

"Thank you for suggesting lunch out here," I said, taking our empty plates. "It was most enjoyable."

He very deliberately raked his gaze down my body to my crotch and he licked his lips. "Oh, I bet it is."

Sparks danced down my spine, warmth pooling in my balls.

This boy—this man—was sent to test me, I was sure of it.

I went inside, only breathing after I'd dumped the plates in the sink and was sitting behind the shield of my laptop. I put my headphones back on and ignored the invisible pull of Benji outside on my balcony. I ignored the pull in my body, the burning want that now seared my veins.

I was pretty sure it was only going to end one way—

with him getting what he wanted from me, being face down on my bed—but I had to be strong.

Even if he was offering . . . and he certainly wasn't being shy about it.

Would it complicate things?

Probably.

But he was only here a week.

I should just enjoy it while I could. And by god, I bet his tiny little arse was sweeter than honey . . .

My phone buzzed, startling me and snapping my thoughts back out of the gutter like an elastic band.

Damn.

It was Perla from the office, and she was sending through some files that needed my attention before close of business.

Perfect.

Distraction and data. Just what I needed.

I had more emails too. More files, more information, more cataloguing and registering.

And, as if Benji sensed I had actual work to do, he left me alone.

Mostly.

He swept the floor, he tidied the kitchen. The smell of lemon disinfectant down the hall told me he even cleaned the bathroom. He read some more of his book. A Stephen King novel, I noticed.

His reading selection pleased me. I wasn't entirely sure why.

He pottered around the kitchen, used the blender,

chopped something, washed something, all while humming and dancing.

He looked so carefree. So happy.

He also looked like sin personified in those too-low sweatpants and his too-short tee shirt. His pale body underneath, his hip bones . . .

He needed to eat more.

I wanted to feed him.

Christ.

I cleared my throat and made myself focus on my screen. Benji appeared at my side with a glass of water and a coaster. "Is your throat okay? You coughed a bit."

He brought me a glass of water . . .

I took my headphones off and slid them onto the table. "I'm fine, but thank you."

"Dinner won't be long. It's five-thirty already."

I double-checked the time on my laptop screen. Shoot. It was that late already?

"You lose track of time so easily," Benji said smoothly. Then he slid his hand along my shoulder and squeezed. "God, you're tense."

I was going to tell him to stop, but he dug his thumb into my shoulder and it felt so damn good. Then he went in with two hands and I could have wept. I closed my laptop and closed my eyes. "Oh god," I breathed. "That feels so good."

"You work too hard," he said, still digging into the meat of my shoulders with his thumbs, then my neck. "You need to unwind more. Relax your body."

It felt so good, so fucking good, I couldn't have asked him to stop even if I'd wanted to.

And I didn't want to.

He stood closer than he needed to, then his hands began to smooth over my collarbones, caresses in between massaging. His soft touch lingering before digging into me again.

"I know what else would help you relax," he murmured, low and seductive. His hand ran down over my pec, fingers skimming over the fabric covering my nipple.

God, he was so good at this.

"You're playing a dangerous game," I said, my voice rougher, breathier than I'd intended.

He leaned down, his nose nudging my nape, and he whispered, "I'm not playing. I told you I was a sexual person, Nolan." His lip skimmed my ear and goose flesh rippled over my entire body. "I like sex. I want it all the time." Then he kissed the side of my neck, that spot below my ear that drove me crazy. "I need it, Nolan."

I stood up, the chair scraping backwards into him. I turned around but he turned my seat and pushed my shoulder. "Sit," he ordered.

I sat, my breath leaving me in a rush, every nerve on high alert, desperate and so turned on.

He smiled as he went to his knees between my legs. "Let me take care of you," he murmured.

Right then, I'd have let him do whatever the fuck he wanted to me.

He palmed my erection through the material,

humming and licking his lips. "Oh my," he breathed. "I need to taste you."

My fingers found his jaw, my thumb swiping his bottom lip. "These lips..."

He smirked as he took my thumb into his mouth, closing his lips around me.

I grunted as I pulled my thumb free. "Tease."

He grinned, licking his lips, and turned his attention to the hard-on in my pants. He pulled the elastic down and pulled my cock out, his hand around the shaft. "Oh fuck, yes," he said with a sigh. "I knew you'd have a gorgeous cock."

Oh fuck.

He leaned in and tongued the frenulum, then kissed the tip. Soft lips opening, his tongue swiping the slit, his big eyes looking up at me.

"You're so fucking beautiful," I grit out.

He opened his lips and took me in, his eyes never leaving mine. His tongue swirled and he hummed as he sucked me down.

My arse almost left the chair, needing more of this ecstasy. I raked my hand through his hair, fisting the curls, desperate to force him down, to take all of me, but somehow finding the restraint not to.

God, how I wanted to.

He groaned when I pulled on his hair, his eyes closing slowly, his lips smiling around my cock.

I slid my other hand along his jaw, framing his face, his neck, as he slid his mouth up and down my cock, his lips wet and slick. He moaned as he took me deep, humming and sucking, hot and wet, and holy fuck, this was bliss.

I hadn't had this kind of attention in far too long.

And he was too good.

Then he cupped my balls and fisted the base, and I was too worked up, too turned on.

"You're gonna make me come," I said. "Those fucking lips."

He smiled, his eyes rolling closed, and took me deeper. He worked me harder, beckoning my orgasm closer and closer.

"Benji," I grated out. "Gonna come."

I tried to pull out, tried to back him off, but he only fought harder to stay, to take it.

I gripped his hair harder then. "You want it, huh?"

He nodded, so I forced him down, sliding into his throat, and he swallowed around me, sucking me like he needed it. Groaning out a pleading sound that ended me.

"Fuck," I bit out as my orgasm ripped through me. I came hard, spurting down his throat, and he hummed, rocking back and forth as he took every drop.

My mind spun, all my senses a jumble of ecstasy and bliss. I was vaguely aware of Benji tucking my dick back into my pants, and when I focused on him, he was smiling like the cat who got the cream.

Literally.

But then he did the darndest thing.

He crawled into my lap, curled himself up, and wrapped his arms around me, his head in the crook of my neck. I had one arm around his back, my other arm around his knees, and damn, if he didn't fit against me like a glove.

I wasn't used to cuddling after sex—not really the done thing in my recent experience of convenient sex and leave—but this . . . I could get used to this.

He sighed, snuggling into my neck more, and I instinctively held him tighter. "Are you okay?" I asked.

He hummed. "Oh yes, very. Do you mind me sitting like this?"

Curled up like a child in my lap?

Couldn't say I'd ever done that before either.

"I like it," I admitted quietly.

"Did you like what I just did to you?"

Oh god . . .

"Very much."

"I liked it too," he whispered.

Then, all too late, I remembered something. "Did you . . . ? I didn't make you come."

Benji sat up then, his bony arse grinding on my thigh, his face incredibly close, his dark eyes like molten onyx. "Oh no, you're going to do that later."

I couldn't believe how certain he was of that. I couldn't even believe he'd said that either, but still . . . "Is that so?"

He nodded, then put his face back into my neck, his voice sweet and matter of fact. "Oh yes. After dinner, you'll take me to bed and fuck me so good."

A wave of heat rushed through me, and my voice came out much rougher than I'd intended. "Oh really?"

He nodded against my neck. "Yes, really. I'll be face

down on your bed and you can rail me however you want."

Sweet mother of god, have mercy.

"However I want?"

How was this even a conversation I was having right now?

"Now I've tasted your cock," Benji said before he let out a long sigh, "I don't want anything else. We should probably discuss sexual health."

Oh shit. "Yes, of course."

I'd been so busy trying to deny this, I'd forgotten the most important part.

"I get tested regularly," he went on to say as if he were discussing the weather. "Last test was two weeks ago. I got my results last week, and I'm all clear. I'd show you the results on my phone, but I don't want to get up right now. And I'm on PrEP."

I rubbed his back. "I was tested a few months back, but I've not been with anyone since. My results are on my phone."

I grabbed my phone and found the email, showing him the results. I had nothing to hide.

He read it, then put my phone down with another contented sigh. "So you can fuck me raw if you want."

Jesus H Christ.

He chuckled, because I'd clearly jolted or froze . . . or maybe he felt my pulse kick in my neck. "Do you want to do that, Nolan?"

Oh my freaking god.

Hell yes, I did. But I also hadn't ever done that before and it was a little daunting, if I was being honest.

"I really need you to come inside me," he whispered, then began to kiss and suckle on my neck, then he reached my ear. He sucked the earlobe in between his lips, then nuzzled his face into my neck again. "Please?"

I'd like to think I had a logical brain; reasonable, perhaps even above average cognitive reasoning skills, analytical, sensible . . .

Yeah.

Benji begging me in that soft, helpless tone, and I had no thoughts at all. I'd give him whatever he damn well wanted.

I pulled back, lifted his chin with my fingers, and crushed my mouth to his. He grunted, smiling into the kiss as he changed position, never breaking the kiss but moving to straddle me instead.

My arms went around him so easily. He was thin, with a slight frame. He weighed next to nothing, and he climbed me like a tree. I had to crane my neck up as he bared his kiss down on me, delving his tongue into my mouth.

He rocked his hips forward, and his sweatpants scarcely hid his erection. I wasn't getting hard again any time soon, but I still wanted him. That burning desire to take him to bed and bury myself inside him never waned.

He smiled and broke the kiss, leaning his forehead to mine. His eyes were dark and full of spark, his lips curved up like the devil. "Fuck, you can kiss," he murmured. "You taste so good, you smell divine, and your cock . . ."

He groaned as he ground down on my sensitive dick, making me hold him still. "And your hands," he purred. "You have big hands. Strong and in control. Fuck, Nolan. You can have me as many times as you want while I'm here. I'm all yours."

His words burned behind my sternum, embers glowing white hot. He had no idea how much I . . .

"Hmm," he hummed, smirking, his voice soft and rough. "You like that, don't you? I can see it in your eyes. Which part, Nolan? That you can have me as often and however you want?" He paused, challenging, teasing. "Or that I'm all yours?"

Then he laughed and licked his lips, his gaze locked with mine. "Mmm," he groaned out, kissing down my jaw so he could whisper in my ear. "That I'm all yours. That's what you like. Your eyes don't lie."

I ran my hands up his back and pulled him down onto me, holding him tight and flexing my hips, desperate to feel more of him. "You have no idea how much I like it," I breathed.

The little minx chuckled, kissing me softly. "Then take me to bed and show me."

I groaned, my dick starting to show some interest.

"What about dinner?" I asked. Pretty sure he'd mentioned that before.

"Dinner can wait. I cannot."

Then I remembered he'd asked me to come inside him . . . yeah, my dick was definitely into that idea. I recalled seeing his backpack full of condoms and lube, and there had been a box of PrEP.

"Are you sure?" I asked. "Do you want me to fuck you bare?"

He pulled back and for the first time there was a flash of insecurity in his eyes. "I don't . . . I don't do that with clients, just so you know. I have protected sex only. It's too risky otherwise." He shrugged. "But I trust you. I can trust you, right?"

I stroked his jaw, soft and reassuring. "I've shown you my health status. I wouldn't lie about that. Bareback is not something I do either, to be honest. Safe sex was drummed into me, and I haven't been in any long-term, committed relationship . . ." I studied his big brown eyes. "But I won't do it if you're unsure."

"I want to try it," he murmured. He climbed off me and a second later was back with his phone. He showed me his results. "I wouldn't lie about it either." He swung his leg over me and straddled me, my hands going to his hips so easily. "I'm not going to get another chance, really. Unless some other rich guy wants to hit me with his car and let me stay at his place for a week." He straightened some strands of my hair. "And I can guarantee if that did happen, he'd never be as sweet as you."

"Sweet?"

He nodded. "Do you know how many men would have used me by now if they were in your shoes? Like, the first day, for sure, and they wouldn't have been nice about it. With you, I had to drop all kinds of hints and pout like a child to get what I wanted."

I chuckled. "So the pouting was a ploy."

"Absolutely. I did it once and your pupils blew out and your nostrils flared, so I knew you liked it."

"So my eyes don't lie, my pupils dilate, and my nostrils flare."

He nodded with a sigh and nestled his face in my neck again. "Yes. Please tell me you don't play poker."

I rubbed his back, and something he said before was still hanging in my mind. "I won't use you," I said quietly. "Like other men."

"You're already nothing like other men," he replied simply. "You treat me like a person."

"You deserve nothing less than that."

"And you still haven't taken me to bed," he added with a long sigh. Then he lifted his head, showing me the most pitiful pout. "All I want is for you to rail me, many times, and you still haven't done it yet. Not even once."

I touched my thumb to his bottom lip. "This pout won't work now you've told me it's fake."

He turned up the dial, pouting like a spoiled child, his puppy-dog eyes large and dark. He was nothing short of an anime character. "Don't you want me? I need you to want me, Nolan."

I groaned and gripped his arse as I stood up, and he wrapped his legs around me. "I'll show you what that pout will get you," I said, carrying him down the hall.

He laughed as he locked his legs around my waist, his arms around my neck, his lips finding mine in a searing kiss.

He was a brat.

And he was about to find out just how much I wanted him.

SIX
BENJI

I DIDN'T WANT to play Nolan like that, but he was so easy. I knew he wanted to dick me. I knew it. He'd been fighting it all day, and credit where it's due, he took some wearing down.

My god, how I wanted him to fuck me.

I thought maybe tasting his dick, being on my knees between his legs and sucking him dry would be all I needed.

But no.

Now I wanted it all.

I wasn't kidding when I'd told him I hadn't gone raw with anyone else. That wasn't a lie. My sex work had a mandatory-condom policy. My regular clients knew that, and if a john objected, he could go find someone else.

But I wanted to try it.

Fitch and Ky loved it, but I'd never been game.

Until Nolan.

He was different. I trusted him. Hell, I *liked* him.

If I woke up in an alternate reality and wasn't a rent boy, and if I'd met Nolan in a bar or in the supermarket, I'd hook up with him. Hell, I'd ask him out for dinner and spend the night at his place, where he would do every wonderful thing to me that I needed him to do.

That he was about to do to me.

He attempted to throw me on the bed, but I clung to him, my legs wrapped around his waist, my arms around his neck. I didn't want to let him go.

He laughed as he knelt on the bed. "I'm gonna need you to let go at some point."

I decided keeping my legs around him was way more fun. I let go of his neck, and as my shoulders hit the bed, his hands held my hips, holding me, rocking me on his hardening dick.

God, I wanted this.

I needed him inside me.

"Fuck yes," I breathed, running my hands over my chest, down my stomach. "We have way too many clothes on."

Grinning, his fingertips slid under the waistband at my sides and pulled my pants off me in one fluid, well-practised move. His eyes went from my hard cock to my eyes. "No underwear," he murmured.

I licked the corner of my lips. "Waste of time."

"Hmm," he hummed, then with delicate fingers, traced the seam of my balls. "Do you want to come before I fuck you, during, or after?"

Oh fuck.

My cock twitched at his words, his touch. No one's

ever asked me about what I want, about my pleasure. "Any of those options sound good to me. All three, if you're good enough?"

He chuckled. "It's not a question of my capabilities, Benji." He leaned over me, his gaze locked with mine, his hand now cupping my balls. "It's about how much pleasure your body can handle."

Heat bloomed in my belly, unfurling through my limbs, making me warm all over.

"I want it all," I whispered. "Any way you want to have me."

His nostrils flared and he squeezed my balls. "You shouldn't say that. Because I want to have you every way possible."

I squirmed under his touch, under the fire of his gaze. My cock was rock hard, his hold on my balls lessened to a pull and roll. "Fuck Nolan, please."

His grin was wicked as he fisted the base of my erection. "Please, what?"

"Please hurry," I said. If he wasn't inside me soon, I was going to lose my freaking mind.

He tsked me, shaking his head. "You said any way I want, not what you want." Then sliding both hands under my arse, he lifted my hips up so he could lick up my shaft. "And I want to take my time and see all the different ways I can make you come."

Oh, holy fuck.

My entire body felt electric and I had no idea what to do with my hands, so I pulled at my hair.

And then he sucked me into his mouth and the wet,

tight slide of his lips, his tongue . . . And the way he held my hips up to his mouth and took me in deep. I was helpless and at his sweet mercy.

"Oh fuck," I gasped. I could seriously come like this. I was racing toward the precipice already. And no one had ever made me come so fast.

Hell, no one had ever made me come, not without my own hand, anyway. Let alone this fast.

Did I want to endure his cock in my arse when I was sensitive after orgasm? Or did I want to draw this out?

"I changed my mind," I blurted out.

Nolan stilled immediately, pulling off my cock. His lips red and wet, his eyes concerned. "Okay."

Sweet Jesus, he thought I changed my mind about the whole thing . . .

"No, I only want to come with your cock in me," I said. "You got me close already and I want you buried inside me when I come."

He grunted and flipped me over. I was a startled mess of limbs and surprise until he gripped my hips again and tongued a stripe over my arsehole. I gripped the bed covers and yelped, but then he drove his tongue into me.

I wanted to touch my cock so badly. I wanted to ease the ache, the urgency . . .

But I needed him inside me first.

"Nolan," I bit out. "Fuck. Please."

He fucked his tongue in and out faster, deeper, his hot breath almost sending me over the edge.

He was torturing me.

It was a myriad of everything wonderful and

agonising desperation. Too much yet not enough, needing it to end and needing it to never stop. Wanting more and not sure I could handle it.

I fisted the bedding and splayed my hips, giving him better access. My cock hung heavy, painfully full, leaking.

I wanted to beg him, to plead, to get mad and lash out. Instead, it came out as a sob. "Please."

His mouth was gone then, and I wanted to wail, to yell, and to weep. But then there was the click of a lube bottle and cool liquid dripped down my crack. Clarity, at last . . . Until he drove a finger inside me.

Oh, fuck yes.

One step closer but not close enough.

With one hand on my hip, he pulled me backwards onto his finger. I rocked back on it, my forehead pressed into the covers. "Please, Nolan. Please."

In all my years as a rent boy, I'd mostly had to take care of prep myself. Most johns didn't want the hassle or the inconvenience. A slap of lube and an intruding finger was all I was usually afforded.

But Nolan was making it part of the foreplay. He was making this good for me.

He was trying to kill me.

I was strung so tight, so desperate, I wasn't sure how much more of this I could take. "Okay, if you don't fuck me right now, I will change my mind again, so help me god, Nolan."

He chuckled. He actually fucking chuckled, and I tried to turn around to give him a piece of my frazzled fucking mind, but he pressed my shoulder down with one hand, held my hip with his other, and the blunt head of his cock met my hole.

"You're so impatient," he said, like he had all the time in the world.

I tried to rear back, tried to take him inside me, but he held my hip with more force now and he leaned over me. He grunted behind my ear, his cock pressing closer, almost . . . so fucking close.

"You said I can fuck you how I want to fuck you," he grit out. "And I want to fuck you slow."

I pressed my face into the soft bed covers and sobbed. That's how much I needed it, and that's how much he was denying me. That I was a sobbing fucking mess resorting to begging. "Please just do it. Please. Please."

Then he pushed into me. Slow and breaching, sliding in, all the way in, every fucking inch. "That what you wanted?" he said, voice strained.

It was sheer perfection and everything I'd needed. The intrusion, the breach. The submission of it. The weight of his body on my back, the way his fingers still bit into my hip, how his breath stuttered.

It melted away the tension, the outside world, all the worries in my mind, until all that remained was this.

Him, me, his cock buried inside me. My body, his pleasure. Giving over that part of me while knowing I was the reason he was so turned on, that I could make him come.

The seduction of it all, that's what I craved.

"You feel so good on my bare cock," he whispered, kissing the back of my neck. "Fuck, you're tight. So hot."

God, yes. He was bare, no barrier between us.

Now I wanted it even more.

"Oh, fuck yes," I moaned, rolling my hips. "Move for me, I want to feel your cock."

He groaned as he began his slow thrusts, his hand leaving my hip now, sliding up and under my shoulder. He held me tight, pinning me to him as he fucked me.

Long and deep.

Perfect.

Pleasure began to bubble and fizz in my bones, building and surging to something I couldn't contain.

But then he lifted me by my shoulders, impaling me on his cock while bringing me up to be seated on his lap.

Oh fuck!

Showers of sparks lit up behind my eyelids and I cried out as he hit my prostate. Nolan grunted as he fucked me. "There it is," he said, voice rough. His hand found my cock and he pumped me, and he was buried inside me, rock hard and totally bare.

I was pinned on him, unable to move, restrained by his strong arms and impaled by his huge cock. Just knowing he was going to pump his seed in me sent me over the edge.

My back arched and I screamed as my orgasm ripped through me. He pumped my cock, grinding up into me and holding me on him . . .

Fuck, I'd never come so hard in my life.

And before I could collapse, before I could slump

from exertion, he forced me back down, my face in the bed covers, while he fucked me harder, faster, his cock impossibly huge.

He gripped the tops of my shoulders and held me down as he drove into me. "Fuck," he bit out. "I'm gonna come inside you."

"Oh fuck yes," I cried out. "Let me feel it."

He slammed in, his body flexing hard as he groaned as he came. I could feel his cock pulse and spill, throbbing inside me with each spurt.

Oh holy fuck.

"Oh my god," I breathed. I could feel it. I could actually feel it.

Nolan cried out, collapsing on top of me. He was panting, trembling, his cock still pulsing. "Oh fuck," he said, rolling his hips. "I don't want to stop."

I hummed and raised my arse for him. "You can stay inside me," I said. There was no need to pull out this time. "Now I know why Fitch and Ky love getting creampied so much."

He barked out a laugh and kissed my shoulder, the nape of my neck. "Hottest sex I've ever had," he said.

A thrill ran through me at his admission. "Same," I replied. "A few first times for me."

He froze for a millisecond. "Oh?"

"First time getting raw dogged," I said. "Which I told you before. But also no one's ever prepped me like that before, and I've never been so desperate for cock that I cried before."

He laughed. "You were strung pretty tight," he said, almost proudly.

"I told you I needed it, and you were a fucking tease."

He chuckled again, kissing my nape before he reluctantly pulled out of me. We both moaned. But then he sat up and spread my arse cheeks. "Mmm."

"Inspecting your handiwork?" I said, wiggling my arse a little.

"Fuck yes," he breathed, his voice rough. "That's so hot." Then he leaned over me again, his words pressed to my ear. "And knowing you have my come in you stirs something primal in me."

Desire and warmth flooded through me again. I liked that we could share this first for both of us. "Good. Because you can do everything you just did to me all week long."

He grunted out a pained laugh. "You know, once upon a time I'd have said I had impeccable self-control." Then he crawled off me and got off the bed. He tapped my arse. "Come on, let's get you into the shower."

Hmm, showering together? Hell yes. I got up slowly, taking stock of any aches or pains, pleasantly surprised to find there were none. The opposite, in fact. I felt so damn good . . .

"So when I said you could fuck me like that all week and you referred to your self-control in the past tense, were you implying that yes, you would be fucking me like that all week? Or is that wishful thinking on my behalf?"

He grinned, his tongue caressing the corner of his mouth. Then he looked at me, mostly naked, with smeared come on my shirt and stomach. He groaned, his nostrils flaring before he put his fingertip to my chin and raised my face to his. "You are a dangerous creature," he whispered. "Here to tempt me, I'm sure."

I pouted and batted my eyelashes a little. "So that's a yes?"

He growled at me, playful with a touch of tortured. "Shower. Now."

"Only if you join me."

He snatched up my hand and led me to the bathroom. It was luxurious, of course, and the walk-in shower was definitely big enough for two. Hell, it'd be big enough for six if we tried. Nolan turned the water on, then turned back to face me.

"I seemed to have come all over my shirt," I said, stating the obvious and playing on his weakness. I bit on my lower lip before pouting. "Oh no. I'll have to be naked all the time."

He laughed and pulled my shirt over my head in one fluid movement. Then he gently tweaked my chin. "You are trouble."

"That also wasn't a no."

"You have other clothes."

"Still wasn't a no." I ran my hand over his chest, broad with a perfect spray of hair, down his abs, past his navel, down to his gorgeous cock.

Even flaccid it was a thing of beauty. Heavy and thick, cut, and a dark pink head.

"God, I could suck you again," I breathed.

He took me by the arm and all but dragged me into

the shower. "Trouble with a capital *T*," he said. Then he soaped me up and washed me down. His hands were strong but gentle, each scrub of my body a firm caress.

I felt cared for. Adored, even.

It was a foreign thing, and one I wanted to both cling to with everything in me and avoid like the plague.

Sometimes it was just easier for a john to get his money's worth and go. Emotions just made a mess of everything. It was why I chose not to feel anything. It was easier that way.

I'd struggled at first. The betrayal and hurt from my family could have sent me on a spiral of destruction. Instead I had turned that sting of betrayal into anger and spite.

Was it healthy?

Probably not. But me living my truest life was all the revenge I needed.

It wasn't exactly difficult to cut them off. I'd hated my father most of my life, especially since my mother died. And my brother . . . well, we were never that close. He was a few years older than me and basically a lapdog to my father.

I was no more than an inconvenience, and my sexuality was a stain on the family name, as my father had told me.

So no, I didn't miss my family. I didn't miss the wealth, the nice house and material things.

I missed my mother.

Nothing and no one else.

"Benji?" Nolan's soft voice brought me back to the

present, in the steaming hot shower with this gorgeous man. "You okay? I lost you there for a second."

"Oh, sure," I said, smiling at him in the stream of water. "I was just thinking about all the surfaces in your apartment you can rail me on."

He rolled his eyes and shut the water off. Then he plucked a towel off the rack and put it over my hair, giving it a quick dry. "I was thinking about food. Are you hungry?"

"Mm."

He stopped rubbing my hair and peeked at me under the towel. "Are you feeling okay? Are you sore? I was pretty rough before."

This sweet, sweet man thought what he'd done to me was rough.

"Nolan," I said. "I feel amazing. Best I've felt in a long time. When I said you are going to rail me on every surface in your apartment, I wasn't joking. Or exaggerating. And it wasn't wishful thinking. It was a fact."

He laughed as he dried himself off. "A fact, huh? Can something that hasn't happened yet be called a fact? Or is it an educated estimation of probability?"

"Well, I can declare, mister smart-arse lawyer," I amended, "with an educated estimation of probability that you are going to rail me on every surface in your apartment."

He tied his towel off with a smirk. "You know, a judge might say your findings are biased, based on your personal desires. Wishing it to be so does not make it so."

I snorted. "Objection, your honour." He laughed and

I tweaked his nipple for good measure. "It's not only based on my personal desires. The counsel wishes for it also."

He hummed happily as he ran his brush through my hair. "You may also need to reevaluate the counsel's ability to rail you on every surface over the next six days. As much as he wishes otherwise, this thirty-six-year-old body can't do what your twenty-one-year-old body claims to require."

Ignoring how sweet it was of him to brush my hair and the warmth his kindness filled me with, I found myself smiling at his handsome face. "Your thirty-six-year-old body is a fucking masterpiece. What you did to me tonight? Utter perfection, and unlike anything I'd had before. So maybe don't be so concerned with the frequency with which you deliver the goods but more so the quality."

He rolled his eyes again, but he looked secretly pleased with what I'd said. He took my hand and led me to the door. "Come on, let's go eat."

"You wanna eat dinner wearing only towels?"

He stopped and shrugged. "We're going to eat dinner, then maybe watch some TV or read a book in bed. Is there any point whatsoever in us getting dressed again?"

He was such a fast learner.

"Absolutely not."

SEVEN
NOLAN

I DIDN'T KNOW what this was.

Apart from the hottest thing I'd ever done, it also felt right.

Benji was fun, sexy as hell, and smart. He was great company—jokes over dinner, dripping with sexual energy, sultry and playful.

And temporary.

Maybe that was why I was enjoying having him around so much.

Because I knew, at the end of the week, he'd be gone. There was no hassle, no repercussions, no commitment, no responsibility.

Just the best sex of my life.

And the reason my heart squeezed and butterflies filled my belly when he laughed. When he swayed his hips as he walked, playing up to me. When he licked his lips and looked up at me through his lashes. When he sat on my lap as we ate dinner, feeding each other and laughing...

Because it was exciting, and the sad truth was I had been lonely.

I would never deny that I enjoyed his company. I enjoyed his sense of humour, his quick wit, his intelligence.

His body.

My god, his body.

We did go to bed, together and naked. He simply decided that he was sleeping in my bed, and I certainly wasn't going to argue. Hell no. His warm body, lithe and limber, curling into me as he fell asleep was amazing.

And waking up to him writhing against my morning wood was... fuck, an incredible way to start my day.

"Morning," I croaked.

"Oh, thank god. About time," he whined, rubbing his arse against my very awake dick.

"What time is it?" I croaked, reaching for my phone. It was almost six thirty.

"Time for you to fuck me again," he whisper-moaned. "If you're going to work today, you need to meet your obligations before you leave."

I chuckled, kissing his shoulder. "My obligations?"

"Yes, you said you'd fuck me as many times as possible." He kept writhing against me, rubbing me, and arching his back. "I've been waiting for you to wake up for so long. Feel this," he said, taking my hand from his hip and running it down to his erection. "See how hard I am for you?"

Warmth and desire rushed through me, heat pooling low in my belly. My cock throbbed between his arse cheeks. "God, Benji," I murmured. "You trying to kill me?"

He stilled, his voice serious. "If you don't fuck me into this mattress right now, I'll seriously consider it."

I chuckled against the back of his neck, giving his cock a long, slow pull as I rutted against his arse, my cock sliding in behind his balls.

"Oh fuck," he breathed, writhing against me, fucking my fist. "Please, do it. I need you inside me, right now."

I rolled him onto his stomach and lay on top of him. "Like this?"

He groaned and spread his legs wide. "Fuck yes."

Then he slid his hand under his hip and tried to rise up a little so he could stroke himself. "Just do it. Put it in me."

Well, I had every intention of doing that but not without lube. I leaned back onto my haunches and snatched the lube off the bedside.

"I said just put it in me," he barked at me over his shoulder.

I ran my hand up his spine to the back of his head and gently held him down. "I'll put it in you when you're ready," I said. "You'll get it soon enough."

He whined again, rolling his hips and stroking his cock. "Please."

My god, he was such a slut for it.

I leaned back again, running my hands down his

back, digging my blunt fingertips in, making him stretch and arch on reflex.

It earned me a moan and made me smile.

I spilled some lube down his crack, working a thumb into his hole. Pushing and kneading, stretching.

Benji bucked up and spread his arse cheeks with both hands. "Jesus, Nolan, I swear to god."

"You're so impatient," I murmured.

"I want it so bad," he mumbled. "I want more of your come in me. Please."

Desire unfurled in me, scorching hot and addictive. My cock leaked precome, aching now, desperate to be in him.

I lubed myself up, put my left hand beside his head, and guided my cock into his hole with my right.

He bit out a stifled cry into the mattress, keeping his arse up for me.

"Is that what you wanted?" I breathed, voice rough.

"Yes," he cried. "Fuck yes."

"God, you're so tight right now."

My cock strained to push deeper. So tight, so hot.

So perfect.

I gripped his hips and sank all the way in. Benji whined, his hands searching for purchase in the sheets. He felt like heaven. I'd never known a bliss like it.

I wanted to stay buried inside him all day long. I wanted to give him nothing but my cock and come all goddamn day. If he wanted it on every surface in my apartment, I'd gladly give it.

As much as he could take, as much as I could give.

Up to the hilt, I pushed my hips in and drove him up the mattress, making us both cry out. And once I began to fuck him, I couldn't seem to stop.

Every thrust in felt better than the one before. The race to the peak of pleasure so intense, so mind-bending. Nothing else existed. Nothing but my cock and his arse.

And he fisted the pillows and took it, moaning with every slam of my hips.

I couldn't have stopped now, even if I'd wanted to.

I was so close to the edge. So close to perfection and ecstasy so pure . . .

And he wanted me to come in him. He needed it. And fuck, there was nothing hotter for me, knowing he'd have my seed in him all day when I was at work. That I'd leave this claim on him, in him.

"Gonna come inside you," I grit out.

"Please, please," he groaned. "Give it to me."

My cock impossibly hard, I slammed into him again, pleasure reaching a breaking point, and toppled over the edge. I held his hips, buried up to my balls inside him, as my orgasm barrelled into me.

Wave after wave rolled through me, intense and consuming. I groaned as I came, pumping my come into him.

He cried out as he took it, his eyes wide, his body rocking with each pulse.

"Holy fuck," he breathed. "Oh my god, Nolan."

I fell forward, collapsing on top of him, panting, head

spinning. I was still embedded in him and had neither the intention nor the ability to move.

"Fuck." I rolled my hips and sensitive jitters hit me.

Benji groaned out a laugh. "I love your cock inside me like this," he breathed. "How am I supposed to survive all day without it while you go to work?"

Work.

I snorted. "Work? I'm not going to work today."

He hummed happily. "Really?"

I hadn't really intended to take a second day off, but now that I'd said it, I was one hundred percent happy to not go. "Really."

"Hmm. Whatever are we going to do all day?"

"I'm going to do exactly what you wanted," I murmured, kissing and biting his shoulder. "I'm going to fuck you on every surface in this apartment."

Benji laughed, his body vibrating as he did, sending exquisite shivers through me from where I was still buried inside him.

I stilled his hip with my hand. "Oh god," I hissed. "Sensitive." I didn't want to pull out of him, but I did, grunting with the onslaught of sensation as I rolled off him.

He hummed as he wiggled his arse, but then he rolled onto his side to face me. His chest and the sheets were covered in his come again.

"You came?" I asked, the words out before my brain could stop them. "I missed that. Sorry."

He smeared it some more, giving me a wicked smile.

"Fuck yes, I came. Like the second you entered me. I told you I needed it."

I laughed, surprised. "You are a little sex imp, aren't you?"

He grinned, his tongue licking his bottom lip. His sleep-messed curls and glittering eyes were a dangerous combination. "I told you I'm a sexual person, Nolan. I love it. And taking you raw, having your come inside me . . ." He closed his eyes and hummed. "And you're gonna do it all day? You're spoiling me."

I scoffed because I wasn't entirely sure he thought he was the one getting spoiled. "You begging for it is spoiling me too."

He preened a little, but then his gaze went down my body. "Hm. How much recovery time are we talking here? You'll need snacks to keep your energy up. Maybe some electrolytes."

I barked out a laugh. "You make it sound like I'm prepping for a marathon."

He gently booped my nose with his fingertip. "Correct." Then he rolled out of bed and sauntered toward the bathroom. "Joining me in the shower?"

I groaned. "I'll need to call my work first."

I heard the shower start, and he called out. "Don't take too long, Mr O'Brien. I'm an impatient man."

I chuckled because, hell yes, he was. And I was ridiculously happy to let him boss me around. I wasn't sure I recognised this version of me.

Calling in sick to work so I could spend the entire day having sex.

The best sex of my life.

But still . . . who was I, and what the hell was I thinking?

I was entitled to paid sick days. But this was out of character for me. So unlike me.

Maybe the thrill of playing hooky was part of the appeal. I felt naughty, like a delinquent. I'd followed every rule, every straight line my entire life. This was new, and exciting. A rush.

It felt good.

I emailed the office a very short and succinct note.

Am unwell today. Apologies. Taking a sick day.

Then I put my phone on silent and followed Benji into the shower.

THE FIRST FLAT surface was the kitchen counter. We'd managed a light breakfast and got as far as cleaning up.

It didn't help that Benji wore nothing but his briefs. At least I'd opted for sweatpants. Both were easy to pull down when Benji had bent himself over the kitchen counter.

I tried to be mindful of his hips and the hard counter edge, but god, putting a second load into him was almost as fast as the first one had been.

He was a siren to me.

His body called to me in ways I'd never known.

The third time was mid-afternoon, on the sofa. Him on his knees facing the balcony with me taking him doggy style, hoping no neighbours could see us, kinda wishing they would.

I wanted people to watch as I fucked him.

Afterward, he lay lengthways on the couch, his briefs still around his thighs. He reached around and gave his arse cheek a wobble. "I'm so full of your seed," he murmured.

I came back with a washcloth, sat on the edge of the sofa, and gently wiped his arse cheeks. "Did you want to have another shower?"

"No. I want to keep it inside me."

Jesus.

"But I probably should. Otherwise I'll make a mess everywhere."

I could not believe this was a conversation we were having.

"Plus," he added, "you can add more later tonight."

I snorted. "I don't know how much more I have left in me."

He chuckled. "Never fear. I'll work it out of you."

Oh my god.

"Need me to help you up on your feet?"

He hummed. "Yes. And I'll need your help in the shower, and I'll need your help drying off and getting dressed. Then I'll need your dick inside me again."

"More?" I helped him to his feet, holding his hand. "I'm going to need to hang an out-of-order sign on my dick."

He smirked. "Oh please. You enjoy this as much as me."

I couldn't deny that. We both knew it.

I thumbed his chin, then his bottom lip. "I do. I haven't had this much sex since college. And never raw."

He hummed, his gaze drawing down to my sweatpants. "It's different, huh? Feels . . . better?"

I nodded. It felt better than better, though I wasn't about to describe how it really made me feel.

Like I had some claim on him now. Like he was mine.

"I might have to come back after this week every time I want to feel this good."

I groaned, thrilling at the idea.

"I wouldn't say no," I admitted.

He purred, giving me a playful smirk. "Hmm."

Before either of us could say something we couldn't promise, I took his hand and led him to the shower. I did join him, enjoying it all too much as I washed him, cared for him. I kissed his shoulder, his nape, as I cleaned him down. I even washed his hair, massaging his scalp, getting lost in the water beads on his eyelashes, at how his lips parted, at the faint freckles on his cheeks.

So fucking beautiful.

I loved how his cock hung heavy, how his lithe body moved, how his Adam's apple moved when he put his head back to rinse the shampoo.

He made my heart flutter.

Which was foolish of me. I knew it was, yet I couldn't help the way I felt. I wanted to protect him. I wanted to keep him here with me. I wanted to hear him laugh, and I wanted to hear him moan when I adored his body with mine.

I wanted him.

Which was impossible.

And so very foolish.

But he was mine for the week he was here, and I had to convince my heart that was enough.

With my hands on his hips, I kissed the back of his head. "I'll go make a start on dinner. Take all the time you need."

I found some clean sweatpants and went to the kitchen. I figured a chicken salad sounded good, so I began prepping it, trying not to overthink everything, and soon after, Benji appeared. He was wearing my dressing gown, open at the front to reveal some briefs, his curls still damp, and he looked so damn good it made my brain short circuit.

He was a mix of grown man and boyish charm. He was so sexy, sultry without even trying.

My ideal type. Perfection in person.

He was holding his phone. "Fitch is on his way over. Hence why I added the robe." He did a twirl. "I hope you don't mind."

God.

"I don't mind at all," I admitted. "It's sexy on you."

That earned me a grin. "Ooh, you like it?" He put his hand on his hip and pretended to walk a catwalk like a model, with a turn and flourish in front of me.

I laughed. "I like it a lot."

This seemed to please him. "Mmm. Then I shall wear it every day I'm here. And nothing else. That way, you can just lift it up," he said, turning around, sliding the robe up to his arse. "Whenever you want a little dip."

"A little dip, huh?"

He grinned, nodding. "Yes, please."

Christ. Every single thing he did and said was sexual, flirty. Dangerous. My well-used dick wanted more. I highly doubted it could fulfil any promises, but it still wanted more.

"You are a dangerous thing," I said, giving his arse a gentle smack.

He laughed just as the intercom buzzed. "Ooh, that'll be Fitch."

He buzzed him through, and a few seconds later, Fitch came in and laughed when he saw Benji. "Okay, Hugh Hefner. Nice robe."

Benji gave him a twirl. "Cool, huh?"

Then Fitch noticed me in the kitchen. "Oh, and shirtless. Please tell me I interrupted something amazing."

I snorted. "Hello again."

"No, you didn't interrupt," Benji said, leading him to the sofa where they sat. "We were taking a small intermission between epic sex sessions, so this is good timing."

Oh god.

Fitch laughed, excited. "Ooh, details, please."

Benji preened. "Well, you know how you've been telling me how tasty creampies are?"

Oh, fucking hell.

Fitch squealed, gripping Benji's arm and jumping in his seat. "I told you! I can't believe you finally did it! How amazing is it?"

I closed my eyes, embarrassment flaming my cheeks.

They were just going to talk about it like that? While I was right there?

"It's the best thing ever," Benji said. "Nolan even took today off work so he could do me all day long."

I put the knife down, and they both turned to me when it may have clanged a little too loud on the marble top. "Sorry," I said.

Fitch chuckled and elbowed Benji. "Mm, and so sexy. Damn." Then he leaned in toward Benji and pretended to whisper. "Can I have some?"

"No," Benji replied before I could. "He's mine."

Well.

Well, then.

That caused something to flare behind my ribs, warm and lovely.

Wow.

I let out a breath and tried to regain some composure. "Fitch, would you like to stay for dinner? I made grilled chicken and salad. There's plenty if you want some."

Fitch glanced at Benji, as if asking for permission, and Benji nodded.

Fitch grinned at me. "I would love to, thank you."

I set the table for three while they chatted quietly. It clearly wasn't a conversation meant for my ears, and that was fine by me.

Even though I wanted to know.

Well, if it involved Benji, I wanted to know.

Nothing else was any of my business.

Even though I liked Fitch—it was impossible to not like him—but I only cared for matters pertaining to Benji.

Because I cared for him.

And the way he'd snipped back at Fitch: *He's mine.*

Yeah, I cared about that a whole lot.

When I had everything on the table, I slipped away into my room and pulled on a T-shirt. Table manners wouldn't allow me to sit with company over dinner when I was half naked.

"Dinner's ready," I said.

They both looked my way and Benji frowned, and Fitch sighed dramatically. "Aww. He put a shirt on."

Benji gave him a shove and they came to the table, Benji sitting closest to me.

I liked that too.

Fitch ate his dinner like he hadn't had anything so good in his life. I was reminded of how Benji reacted to eating proper food when he first got here, and it reminded me that, all their jokes aside, these boys didn't have an easy life.

"There's more if you want it," I offered.

"This is so good," Fitch said. Then he shook his head at Benji. "You are the real-life *Pretty Woman*."

Benji laughed as he chewed his mouthful, then explained. "I told him I watched it."

"As a ploy to get you to fuck him," Fitch added.

Benji gave him a sharp elbow, but I chuckled. "It worked. Well, the pout worked when he was sad that I wouldn't be his Richard Gere."

Fitch seemed to find this amusing. "Sucker for a pout, huh?"

I couldn't believe I was having this conversation. "Apparently."

"So the leap from pout to creampies was a short one," Fitch said, earning himself another elbow from Benji.

"Dude."

They ate in silence for a bit, and I couldn't stop my curiosity about their earlier quiet conversation. "So," I hedged. "What's news on Oxford Street?"

Benji froze for a second, and Fitch shrugged. "Nothing new. Same old."

Something had definitely happened. Benji's reaction told me enough. "Did the men who chased Benji the other night return looking for him?"

"No," Benji said.

"Yes," Fitch said at the same time.

"Fitch," Benji hissed at him.

"What?" he cried. "I'm not gonna lie to him when he could let you stay here a few more days."

I wasn't sure what to do with this information. I had no problem with Benji staying if he needed to, but it wasn't a permanent solution.

"Is there something I can help with?" I tried instead. "If these men are harassing you—"

"No." Benji shook his head. "It's fine."

"There are laws to protect you."

Benji shook his head again, and Fitch looked like he wanted to say something but couldn't.

"I know going to the police seems—"

"No," Benji said, sharper this time. Then he tried to give me a smile. "It's fine. They'll go away."

"What do they want?" I tried. "You know, in my line of work, I see this kind of stuff all the time. I've learned to never judge anyone for actions under circumstances I myself have never been in." I looked squarely at Benji. "Are they after money?"

His gaze shot to mine and he shook his head. "No. Look, can we drop it, please? It's not important. They'll go away."

I knew if I pushed, I'd only push Benji away, so I let it go. "You can stay here longer," I said. "If it's a safety issue. I don't mind." Then I thought I should clarify something. "And that doesn't have to include our other arrangement. I don't expect anything—"

"It better," Benji said bluntly. "If I'm staying longer, which I'm not, at this point, just so you know. It won't be necessary. But thank you for the offer. Hypothetically though, if I do stay, our agreement of much and thorough fucking will need to honoured."

Fitch snorted. "Priorities."

Benji smiled as he stabbed some chicken and salad and they continued to eat, the conversation about their troubles seemed to be over.

I had the rest of the week with Benji, at least, so maybe we could talk about this again. When we knew each other a little better.

When he trusted me some more.

When we actually got around to having a conversation instead of endless sex.

I felt bad for never pushing him for more information, more conversation.

I believed him though, when he said it wasn't money or drugs.

So what these men were after Benji for, I could only guess. But for now, I'd let it go.

I left Benji and Fitch to chat at the dining table while I cleaned up after dinner, and I was stacking the dishwasher when the intercom buzzed. Benji's gaze shot to mine. "Expecting someone?"

"No," I said, wiping my hands on a tea towel, walking to the door. I checked the screen. "Shit."

"Who is it?" Benji asked. There was alarm in his tone, so I gave him a smile.

"A friend of mine."

"Should we go . . . hide?" Fitch asked.

I buzzed Dominic through and shook my head. "Nah, it's fine."

I should have texted Dominic during the day. I should have let him know I was okay.

I was sure Dominic would, after the initial shock, probably laugh at me. This last weekend was so wildly out of character for me. Me, Mr strait-laced, goody two shoes had spent the last few days holed up with a hooker after a very close call with my car.

We'd be laughing about this over drinks at 180 next week, I was sure of it.

Plus, I'd be lying if I said part of me didn't want someone to know of the crazy sex-filled ordeal.

I opened the door as Dom was knocking on it,

surprising him a little. "Hey. So, you are alive," he said, walking in. "Two days off in a row and . . ."

His words trailed off and he stared at the two guys sitting at my dining table.

That wasn't even the craziest part.

Because Fitch stood up, eyes wide, and he began to smile. "Dom," he said.

"Fitch," Dom whispered. Then he turned to me, shock clear on his face. "What the fuck is going on?"

EIGHT
BENJI

I HAD no clue who Dom was. He was mid-forties at a guess and handsome in a way that wealth allowed—a fitted, tailored suit and expensive shoes. He seemed kinda familiar, like maybe I'd seen him on Oxford or Wylde Street . . .

Oh.

The man who had led Nolan away from me and shoved him into the exclusive club 180.

Fitch clearly knew him.

The way he'd stood up as soon as Dom walked in. Obviously one of his regulars, or a favourite at least.

Dom didn't seem pleased at all to see Fitch. Well, not Fitch himself. He wasn't pleased to see Fitch at Nolan's.

Nolan closed his door and sighed as he walked into his kitchen. "Can I get you a drink? Looks like we could all use one."

Nolan didn't wait for an answer. He pulled a bottle

of whisky down from the cabinet above the fridge, then two glasses. He glanced over at us. "You guys want one?"

I shook my head, and when Fitch didn't reply, I answered for him. "None for us, thanks."

Dom stood unmoving at the door, still trying to process. "So you're not sick," he said to Nolan.

And I didn't much care for that.

I don't know why I felt the need to defend Nolan or shield him in any way I could, but I found myself going to him. I stood next to Nolan, between him and Dom, and touched his waist.

It calmed me, oddly enough.

"You okay?" I murmured to him.

His eyes met mine and he nodded, smiling a little. "It's fine."

"So your name is actually Dom," Fitch said. "I thought it was a title or a status." He walked over to Dom. "You look hot as fuck in that suit. My god. Order me to my knees right now—"

Dom put his hand up in a stop fashion. He closed his eyes and shook his head. "I'm going to need someone to start explaining what's going on here." Then he finally looked at Fitch. "Is he . . . paying you?"

Fitch hummed out a laugh. "Oh no. Not me. I'm just here for moral support. That guy over there belongs to Nolan."

I gave him a wave, though I was sure he could probably tell who I belonged to by how closely I was standing to Nolan, with my hand still on his side.

"No one belongs to me," Nolan mumbled.

That stung to hear. While I technically didn't belong to him, I also kinda did. For this week, anyway. For as long as he was fucking me without a condom, I most certainly did.

Nolan rubbed my back before collecting the two whiskies, walking over to Dom, and handing him one. "Take a seat. I'll explain everything."

They sat on the sofa, body language stiff and closed off, while I took Fitch out onto the balcony. It was getting dark, the air was warm, the night still young.

"Friday night," I heard Nolan begin, "I was drunk and you told me not to drive . . ."

So he was telling him the whole thing.

I slid the door closed, giving them privacy, and when I turned, Fitch was grinning at me. "Are you fucking kidding me? Do you know who that is?"

"No. But you clearly do."

He nodded, excited. "That's my Dom."

"Your Dom?"

"Yes. Well, I wasn't aware it was his real name. When he introduced himself as that, I just assumed we were role playing, ya know?"

"I gathered that," I replied. "You offered to go to your knees in Nolan's living room."

Fitch laughed, so very pleased. "And I would have. I'm telling you, Benj. He is so fucking hot. He goes all daddy-mode and I fucking love it. I thought he just liked being in control, ya know? Like he was the Dom and I was his little sub-boy."

I snorted. "Yeah, and I can tell how much you hate that."

He laughed again. "Lord, the things I've let him do to me."

Jesus.

"So, do you reckon they work together?" he asked.

I nodded and half shrugged. "I guess so."

Fitch studied me for a second. "And what about you, going over to stand with your man."

I snorted and shook my head at myself. "Jesus Christ, Fitch. He's spoiling me. I'll be fucking ruined. How am I supposed to go back to my old life after this?"

Fitch frowned. "You like him."

I rolled my eyes, kinda mad at myself for admitting it, even to myself. "He's . . . He's a good man. Decent, kind. Sexy as fuck."

"And you let him finish inside you," he whispered.

"Was that a mistake?"

Fitch shook his head. "No. Just enjoy it. Enjoy every minute while you have it. He did say you can stay longer if you need to."

"I can't stay here forever," I said, my heart already heavy. "I'm ruined, I'm telling you. Beautiful place, great food, perfect man." I let out a long sigh. "And he's paying me. I mean, what the hell?" I put my hand to my forehead. "I already don't want to leave him, Fitch."

He frowned, sadness replacing his usual upbeat demeanour. "Babe, I'm sorry. But you'll be okay. When all this is over, when those fucking henchmen disappear, you can come back and we'll be hanging out in all our local hangouts. Laughing and carrying on just like old times. I miss you; I hope you know. Just hanging out and stirring shit. I miss the sound of you laughing. Even the apartment seems dull without you."

I sighed and gave him a hug. "I'll be back. I can come back tomorrow if you want?"

"Fuck no. I don't miss you that much."

I laughed and gave him a shove. "How's Ky?"

"He's fine. He's got a date with his two daddies tomorrow night, so he's stoked."

"Mid-week now too?"

Fitch rolled his eyes. "He's not complaining, believe me."

I chuckled and it ended with another sigh. "Do you think they're done talking in there?"

"Probably. Should we go check? I wasn't going to work tonight, but honestly, it's like fate intervened and delivered Dom right to me."

I laughed as the door opened. Nolan poked his head out. "You guys can come in if you want."

I went to him, surprising myself by how easy it was to touch him as I walked past. Surprising myself even more by how much I needed the reassurance of his touch, his closeness.

Fitch, on the other hand, walked in on a mission. Dom was still sitting on the sofa, and Fitch went to his knees in between Dom's legs and he peered up at him, batting his eyelashes. "Please take me home with you," he said.

Dom cleared his throat, embarrassed, and pulled Fitch up by his arm. "Christ, get up."

Fitch went willingly, crawling into Dom's lap, resting his head on Dom's shoulder. "Sorry, daddy."

It was one thing to hear about all his stories, it was another to watch him in action.

Dom huffed and picked Fitch up and plonked him onto the couch beside him. "Behave."

Nolan was staring at them, trying to hide how stunned he was, trying not to laugh. I poked him in the side, burying my smile into his shoulder.

Dom got to his feet, flustered. "I should go."

Fitch stood up too, his puppy-dog eyes in full effect with a brattish pout. "If you won't take me to your place, you can drive me to mine."

Dom huffed again, and I couldn't tell if he was legitimately mad or just pretending to be. "Fine."

Fitch looked at me and grinned as if he'd won first prize. "Bye."

Nolan saw them to the door. "I'll see you at work tomorrow."

Dom gave a nod. "Yes, you will." That sounded more like an order for Nolan to not miss another day. Fitch took Dom's hand and tried to pull him out the door. He scowled. "He's a . . ."

"He's a brat," I offered.

Dom gave a nod in my direction. "Nice to meet you, Benji."

Then he and Fitch were gone, and Nolan closed the door after them. He turned to face me and leaned against the door. "So," he said slowly. "Not how I expected our evening to go."

"Me either. You told him everything?"

He nodded. "Yep. Everything."

"The part about you paying me and us fucking like little creampie bunnies?"

He laughed. "Well, he assumed sex was part of the equation. I didn't feel the need to go into such details."

"But you're going to work tomorrow?"

He nodded. "I have to. We have meetings and I need to be there."

I sighed sadly. "Then you'll just have to make up for lost time before work and again, several times, when you get home."

He laughed. "Haven't you had enough today?"

"Absolutely not."

He held out his hand, so I went to him, threading our fingers. It was such a simple but overrated gesture. For all the sexual things I'd done, holding hands wasn't on the list.

"Let's watch something," he said, pulling me onto the couch with him.

He was on his back, lying lengthways, with me between his legs, my head on his chest. His arm went around my shoulders, and he scrolled Netflix for a while before settling on a comedy series.

It was nothing but background noise to me, something for my eyes to look at while he held me. He traced patterns on my back, his heartbeat thumped in my ear, and I'd never, ever felt so content.

Happy.

I wanted to ask him questions, about Dom, about what he'd said, any questions he'd asked. But this was too good, too perfect to ruin with chatter that might spoil the mood.

I'd never had the comfort of another man's arms for the sake of comfort. I'd never had someone hold me like this. Or lay on a couch together watching TV. It was a couple thing to do. Boyfriends, even.

And I'd never had that either.

Never.

It filled me with something warm and fuzzy, sweet and addictive.

I'd miss this when it was over.

I'd miss him. Nolan, this utterly perfect man.

His strong arms, his kindness. Sure, his dick and the way he cared for me when he fucked me. But I'd miss his smile too. And his scent.

Damn.

I was ruined for my old life.

Going back was going to suck so bad.

"You okay?" Nolan asked quietly.

"Yep. Just thinking."

"About?"

I didn't want to bring the mood down, so I went with funny. "About Fitch and seeing him being a damn brat."

Nolan chuckled, the rumble loud in my ear, my face vibrating on his chest. "He is a brat. God, what are the odds that Dominic knew him?"

"I know," I replied. "Fitch had told me of the older

guy he loved getting railed by. Crazy that you'd know each other." Then I sighed. "He'll be getting railed so hard right now. Well, I hope he is. For his sake. He'll be all sulky if he isn't."

Nolan laughed again and gave the top of my head a kiss. "Like you. No wonder you and Fitch are such good friends."

"I might have sulked, but I'm not a brat."

"No, you're not," he murmured, his tone soft.

I lifted my head to look at him. "What did Dom say? About what you told him."

"He said I was an idiot for drink driving. And he's not wrong. He said paying you to take a week off work was the least I should have done."

"I like him."

Nolan grinned. "He said I needed to not let my sexual desires impede on my work. A day off for legitimate reasons is fine, but so I could stay home and fuck all day . . ." He sighed. "Not so much."

I frowned at him. "Hmm. Maybe I don't like him so much."

Nolan smiled warmly, his thumb finding my chin, my bottom lip. "He's not wrong. I do need to go to work tomorrow."

I sighed dramatically. "And that's fine. But the terms and conditions were that you met all other obligations before and after work."

His smile became a grin, until he drew his bottom lip between his teeth. "Is this you being a brat?"

I laughed and shook my head. "God no. Brattish

really isn't my style, unless it's pouting to get what I want."

"Of course."

So I pouted. "So... about those terms and conditions."

"Before work tomorrow, not tonight."

I pouted harder and he pulled my bottom lip down with his thumb. "It won't work again."

I leaned up some more and looked down at where his crotch was pressing against my stomach. "Oh well, I'll just have to help myself."

He cracked up laughing but slung his legs around my back, holding me so I couldn't get to his dick.

I drove my hips up, pressing my dick against his balls. "Mmm," I said, looking down at him, rubbing myself against him. "I'll do it if you want me to."

He made a low sound. "I haven't done that in years. Like twenty years."

"Didn't like it? Or was it with the wrong person?"

"Maybe both. It wasn't a great experience and I was young. He was older."

I sighed. "No excuse. You're older than me, yet you take very good care of me."

He smiled.

"Like, you're *almost twice* my age."

He gasped and I laughed, then he shot up and grabbed me, flipping me onto my back and pressing his weight down between my legs.

"No jabs about the age," he said, aiming for stern, but his smile won out.

I pulled his face in for a kiss. "I was just kidding, but if you feel the need to punish me . . ."

He growled at me. "You know, I think punishment for you is no sex."

I gasped this time, in absolute horror. "You wouldn't."

He grinned, victorious. "Ah, so that is your Achilles heel."

"Baby, you could get me to do anything in the world your heart desires if the reward is you fucking me. Anything. Literally anything."

He hummed out a chuckle, his eyes sparked with a wicked gleam. "Anything? Baby?"

That made me laugh. "If you promise to leave for work tomorrow with my arse open and full of come, just name it. There's plenty of surfaces in this apartment we haven't tried yet."

"WHAT?" Fitch asked in disbelief. "He asked for what?"

Me, Fitch, and Ky were sitting on Nolan's veranda. It was eleven thirty, the sun was perfectly warm, and the three of us were lounging about, soaking it up like cats.

"I told him I would do anything. Literally anything," I repeated. "I said the words 'if he left me with my arse open and full of his come,' I would literally do any single thing he asked." I sighed. "And there I was, lying ruined on his bed at seven o'clock this morning, and he came out all showered, dressed hot as fuck in his suit, knelt on the bed so he could kiss me, and told me all he wanted was for me to have a good day."

Fitch's face was one of horrified disbelief, and Ky burst out laughing.

"You like him," Ky said. "And it sounds like he feels the same."

"There are no feelings," I said. Then I amended, "On his behalf, anyway. This is purely transactional."

Ky closed his eyes and lifted his face to the sun. "Maybe it started out that way. But it doesn't sound that way now."

I sighed because no, it couldn't be. I couldn't bring him into my world anyway, even if it was true. "He's just a nice guy."

Ky, still with his eyes closed, waved his hand back to the apartment. "Correction. A super rich nice guy. A nice guy who lets you stay in his luxury apartment. Who's paying you to stay in his luxury apartment. I mean, what in the actual Disney movie fuck?"

Fitch snorted. "Pretty sure Disney don't make X-rated movies." Then he turned to me. "But he did leave you with your arse full of his seed, right?"

I laughed. "You're such a whore."

He grinned at me with no shame. "I know, thank you."

"And how did your night end up?" I asked him. "With Mr I-didn't-know-your-name-was-actually Dom?"

Fitch laughed and arched his back with a moan. "So good."

"Did you get the punishment you were begging for?"

"Oh, did I ever." He sighed. "He dropped me home this morning on his way to work."

"You stayed the whole night?"

"Fuck yes, I did," he said. "His place is even nicer than Nolan's, just so you know. And he's not a Dom, but when I call him daddy—" Fitch snapped his fingers. "—something switches on in that man, lemme tell you."

I chuckled. "Did he pay you? Because it sounds like you should be paying him."

Fitch grinned, closing his eyes to the sun. "He did pay, yes. But honestly, I would do it for free. Don't tell him that though."

Ky laughed. "Such a whore."

"Like you can talk," Fitch said. "I can only handle one. How the hell do you handle two daddies?"

Ky smirked. "With servitude and pleasure."

I snorted. "Whore."

He preened. "Thank you."

We were quiet for a moment, then Fitch turned his attention to me. "And Nolan's okay with us coming over today?"

"Yep. I asked him when I got Ky's text this morning. He said it was fine."

"And your Nolan and my Dominic work together?" Fitch pressed.

My Nolan . . .

"I think so. I don't ask for details. Why?"

"Just curious."

Hmm. "You like him?"

He shot me a deadpan stare. "If he asked me to stay

for a week at his amazing place so I could live in the lap of luxury in between him fucking me into oblivion every chance he gets, and if he was paying me for this privilege?" He raised an eyebrow. "I certainly wouldn't be saying no. I'd even let him hit me with his car."

I snorted again. "I didn't *let* him hit me with his car."

"How is your back anyway?" Ky asked. "Fitch said you were all scratched up."

"I'm fine. I just had a sore muscle, but that got ironed out pretty quick."

"I bet it did," he said. Then he sighed. "So, about the guys who were chasing you that night . . ."

I sighed. "Can we not talk about them? They'll go away eventually. They always do."

Fitch shook his head. "Not until he stops looking for you."

"He can fuck off. I hope he rots in jail."

"Do you think he'll get out?"

"Probably. He keeps getting let off because he doesn't do the dirty work. He has his idiot guard dogs on his payroll to do it for him."

Ky turned onto his side to face me. "I don't understand why he won't just give up. It's certainly not out of love."

"It's about control," Fitch said.

I nodded. "Yeah. He hates that he can't control me anymore," I said. "But I also know shit, and the fact he no longer has me on a leash means I'm a loose end."

"I hate him," Fitch mumbled.

I snorted. "Take a number. There is a very long list of people ahead of you."

I hated that they worried for me, and I hated that they had to always be on the lookout for me. It wasn't fair. And I hated that they were also in the firing line because of me.

Anyone being on my father's radar was never good.

But I hated that we couldn't even enjoy a moment in the sun in a super nice apartment without my troubles being a dark cloud over us.

"Enough about that arsehole. You guys hungry?" I asked, trying to lighten the mood. "I can make you some lunch?"

Fitch patted his stomach. "Mmm, food. Whatcha got?"

"Let's go inside and have a look. Fair warning though. It's probably going to be healthy."

I made us each a sandwich full of fresh ham and every salad item in the fridge. Coupled with a glass of juice, if the speed in which Ky and Fitch both annihilated theirs, I assumed it was all pretty good.

"What's your plans for tonight?" I asked them both.

"Work," Fitch said, and Ky nodded.

"What about you?" Ky asked.

"I don't know what time Nolan will be home. So I'll make him dinner and probably spend a good amount of time douching in the shower so he can fuck me all night long."

Fitch laughed. "Look at you being such a perfect househusband."

"I only have a few days left, so I plan to make the most of it."

"Live it up while you can, huh?" Ky nodded. "I get that. Miss your stupid face at home though."

"I miss you guys too."

Fitch looked around the apartment. "No offence, but if I were in your shoes right now, I wouldn't miss your stupid faces one bit."

Both Ky and I laughed, because out of all of us, he'd miss us the most.

NOLAN GOT HOME JUST after seven. I'd cleaned the apartment, read more of my book, watched stupid real estate shows on TV, and cooked us dinner. Just a simple pasta with a side salad, but I was feeling good about myself.

I wanted to be helpful to him. I wanted him to not have to worry about anything after his long day at work.

Fitch's good-little-househusband comment came to mind, and I couldn't even bring myself to care.

Nolan came in and slid his messenger bag onto the sideboard just as I was setting the table. "Hey," he said, smiling at me.

"Hey, you," I said, putting the table caddy of salad dressings down and pulling out his chair. "Come and take a seat. Dinner's done."

He chuckled and sat down, and I was quick to throw my leg over him, sit on his lap with my arms around his shoulders. His arms slid around me and up under my shirt. "You wear this short shirt to tease me, don't you?"

"Absolutely. I'm tempted to take some scissors to it to make it into a true crop top." I pressed my lips to his. "I've done everything I can think of. Cleaning, the apartment and myself, very thoroughly, if you know what I mean. And dinner. I want you to come home and have nothing to do but me."

He hummed happily. "Very thoroughly, huh?"

I nodded. "Fitch said I was a very good househusband. Cooking, cleaning, sex whenever you want. Even when you don't want it."

He laughed, his hands sliding down to my hips. "That's the problem though. Because I always want it."

I ground down on him, feeling his hardening dick, and kissed him. "Glad to hear that. Now, did you want to eat dinner with a hard-on or without?" I leaned my elbows back onto the dining table and arched my back. "You haven't fucked me on your table yet."

He gripped my hips and rose up to grind harder against me. "You are so wicked," he murmured. "All I could think about all day was coming home to you."

"Coming in me," I said, arching my back.

His nostrils flared and I knew dinner was a lost cause. He picked me up and sat my arse on the dining table, kissing me deep. His mouth and hands, his erection and my own aching need to have him fill me up.

I was kicking myself that I hadn't thought to bring the lube out. "Fuck, lube," I said breathlessly. "Just fuck me without it."

He snatched the small bottle of olive oil from the table caddy. "No need," he said, ripping my sweatpants down to my thighs and folding my legs up.

Then he unzipped himself, opening his suit pants and pulling out his eager cock. He slicked himself with the oil, sparing me a mere swipe before he pushed his cock into me.

No prep, no stretching, no warning.

He drove all the way in, holding my legs. I couldn't even arch my back to alleviate the intrusion. His fingers dug into my thighs as he reached the hilt. I was so full of him, unable to do anything but take all of him.

It burned and it was all too much. It was glorious.

He groaned, his face tortured. "Fuck, I'm sorry," he rasped. But then he pulled my arse closer and leaned over me more, pushing deeper. "That's how much I needed you," he bit out. He slid back a little only to thrust back into me. "That's how much you turn me on."

Oh fuuuuuck yes.

"All day," he said. "All I've thought about, all fucking day, is you."

"God, Nolan," I grated out. "Your cock is right where it belongs."

His eyes rolled back and he thrust into me, hard and sharp. Perfect. "Fuck, I'm gonna come already," he said with a groan.

That feeling of elation, of pure fucking bliss, washed over me. Being the reason for his pleasure was a different kind of joy for me.

"Give it to me," I begged. "Please."

He held my legs, my arse at the edge of the table, and every inch of his cock buried inside me, and he threw his head back and came with a roar.

I felt every pulse. Every throb and every spurt.

Warmth rushed through me. Not sexual but something deeper, something else.

I made him happy and he made me his.

It was something new to me. Something completely foreign and I couldn't put a name to it.

It was something wonderful.

He collapsed on top of me. His forehead pressed to my chest as he caught his breath. I raked my fingers through his hair, and I hated that empty feeling when he pulled out of me.

"Are you okay?" he asked. "I'm sorry. That was rough and uncalled for."

He stood up, his eyes haunted. I grabbed his tie so he couldn't go far. "I'm so fucking good right now," I told him, my eyes locked on his. "That was hot as hell."

"I was rough and impatient." He frowned as he tucked himself away. "Did I hurt you?"

"If you hurt me, I'll tell you, and probably kick you in the nads. Just so you know."

He relented a small smile. "That'd be fair."

I sat up, slid off the table, and pulled up my sweatpants. I pulled on his tie again and brought him in for a kiss. "That was hot. I feel . . ." I still couldn't quite name how I was feeling, so I sighed instead. "I feel amazing right now. So no pity party, okay? You showing me how turned on you were for me was possibly the hottest thing you've ever done to me. You can show me like that anytime you want."

He still looked a little troubled.

I took his chin between my thumb and forefinger and brought his nose to mine. "If you kill my buzz, Nolan, I'll be pissed. If it makes you feel any better, I'll let you suck my dick later, okay?"

He smiled then. "Okay."

I leaned in and kissed him softly. It was so easy, so natural. Such a rush. "Let's have dinner and you can tell me about your day."

He helped me serve it up and bring it to the table. "Meetings all day," he said. "Not much to tell. Very boring."

"Did you see Dominic?" I asked.

"Only briefly. We didn't get a chance to chat. He's busier than me. He was in court most of the day."

"Oh? What for?" Then I remembered that these guys were the lawyers, not the ones being charged. "Oh yeah. You guys are the plaintiffs. I forgot. I hear the word court and my mind goes to the ones arrested."

Nolan chuckled. "Ever been arrested before?"

"Nope. You?"

He shook his head. "I'm a good boy."

I snorted. "Objection, your honour."

He laughed. "Sustained." He ate some more. "How was your day? Fitch and Ky came over?"

"Yep. We sat out on the balcony, lounging in the sun like cats. I made them a sandwich. Hope that was okay."

"Yeah, it's fine. Lounging sun cats need sandwiches."

God, he was so cute. "Then Fitch told me he spent the entire night at Dominic's place getting thoroughly railed. He dropped him home on his way to work."

Nolan seemed a little surprised by this. "Good for them."

"Did you know he has the whole daddy thing going on?"

"No, I did not." He made a thoughtful face. "I knew he liked twinks, so I can't say I'm shocked."

"You seemed surprised."

"Surprised that Fitch stayed all night." Nolan smirked at me. "Dominic doesn't typically do that. He likes his privacy."

"Well, Fitch is special," I allowed.

Nolan chuckled. "And what about Ky? You don't talk of him often."

"Ky's great. He's quieter. He's a bit older than me and Fitch. He's twenty-five. Been working the street since he was twenty-one. But he's like us. No drugs, stays out of trouble. Just wants to live his life, ya know? He likes what he does."

"Like you and Fitch," he said. It wasn't a question. I'd told him before we enjoyed our work. Most people didn't understand that, and this was the first time Nolan had questioned it.

"Yep. It can be bad out there. It can be dangerous. I don't dispute that. Some sex workers hate their jobs, hate their lives. They look for escapes in drugs, usually, and end up a statistic."

"I can see how that could happen," he said quietly.

"But Fitch, Ky, and me have each other. We have our apartment. We look out for each other."

"I'm glad." Nolan gave me a sad smile. "So is it something you think you'll do forever? What are your plans for the future?"

I almost snorted. "Future?" I shook my head, smiling at the naivety of such a simple question. "That's subjective, isn't it?"

His gaze cut to mine, narrowing and serious. "No."

"I think your definition of future and my reality of what the future holds are two very different things."

He stared at me for a long moment before he set down his fork. His eyebrows knitted and he spoke in a whisper. "Benji, please don't say that. Everyone deserves a future. Everyone. Whatever hopes and dreams they have, no matter their circumstances. No life is worth more than another."

I found myself smiling at him. He was such a sweetheart, truly believing in the greater good. I reached out and slid my hand over his. "I know. I didn't mean to sound so . . . bleak. It's just . . ." I shrugged. "Sometimes it's hard to picture a future. Like in six months or two years, sure. I can see myself still being where I'm at. But in ten years from now?" Now I sighed. "No. Well, I hope not, anyway."

"Where do you want to be in ten years then?"

"Alive. At least."

Nolan looked as if I'd slapped him. "Benji," he whispered, shaking his head. Christ, were those tears in his eyes? "Please don't talk like that."

I pushed my plate away, my appetite for food now gone. "I don't know where I could possibly be in ten years from now. It's all hypothetical anyway, so what does it matter?"

"Because you matter," he said sharply. "You matter to Fitch and Ky." He swallowed hard. "And you matter to me."

His words hit me like a truck.

I couldn't speak. I didn't know what I was supposed to say to that. My heart was thumping, my mouth suddenly dry.

I mattered to him.

He cared about me.

And for what? What could possibly come from this?

Nothing.

"Nolan," I whispered.

He laughed, an unhappy sound. "It's fine. Just please don't say it doesn't matter. Because it does. And if you want to think about any hopes or dreams you thought you had to forget, or where you want to be in ten years, then please tell me. And we'll see what we can do. Some plan of action to put into motion. I don't know. You have to have something in the back of your mind. Something you always wanted to do. Something that made you sad when you realised you had to abandon it."

I shook my head. "I never had any dreams about what I wanted to be or dream jobs, if that's what you're asking," I said quietly. "Growing up, the only thing I wanted to do was leave home. To be free."

His gaze lasered into mine.

"And now I am," I said, trying to smile for him. "I'm free to be myself. That's all I ever wanted."

Nolan sagged with a sigh. "God, Benj, I'm sorry. Your family . . ."

This was dangerous territory.

"Weren't nice people," I said. I really needed to change the subject. "So no, there was no grand desire for any career. I just wanted a job of my own, my own money, to live my own life. And that's what I'm doing. I told you I liked what I do, and I mean it."

He slid his hand over mine and squeezed. "And I'd never change that. If it's who you are and what you want, then I'm happy for you." He inhaled deeply. "I just hope the you ten years from now is as happy as you are today. With whatever he chooses to do."

I couldn't help myself. I got up and sat on his lap, giving him a hug before kissing his cheek. "Has anyone ever told you that you are the sweetest man to ever live?"

He chuckled, but he leaned into me and we sat like that for a while. Then we cleaned up the kitchen, moving around each other with the occasional soft touch. We watched TV in bed, and he was quick to pull me into his arms, my head on his chest as we laughed at some awesomely bad sci-fi show from the '80s.

He'd said I mattered to him, and lying there with him like that, I could have let myself believe it.

NINE
NOLAN

I WAS SITTING at my desk at work, staring into space and not even seeing any of the files and reports on my desk. My mind was at home, in my bedroom, to be exact, remembering and reliving exactly what I'd done to Benji before work.

My god, his body was utter perfection. As if he'd been designed with me in mind.

His perfect arse, his pretty eyes, his full lips. The way he laughed, the way he clung to me. The way he begged me.

Men had fought wars for less.

I was all too aware I had feelings for him and painfully aware that he was leaving in a few days.

I could ask him to stay longer. Hell, I'd pay him to stay.

But to what end?

I couldn't expect him to stay forever. I couldn't pay

him forever. And I couldn't ask him to quit his job for me. That was ludicrous and unfair on him.

He'd said twice now that he enjoyed his work and that he was an incredibly sexual person. I could vouch for that.

But I couldn't ask him to quit. As much as I wanted him to.

As much as the thought of another man touching him pained me . . .

A sharp knock on my door surprised me, and Dom stuck his head in. "Got a second?"

He had a manila folder in his hand, so assuming it was work related, I nodded. "Sure. Of course, come in."

He did, closing the door behind him, which wasn't protocol . . .

So this was a personal conversation then.

"You were a million miles away," Dom said, sitting across from me. "In a fairly pleasant place, by the looks of it."

I couldn't help but smile. He knew about Benji, so I didn't have to hide it from him. "Something like that. How about you? A little birdie told me his bratty friend stayed all night long at your place the other night."

"Hmm." Dom's eyes met mine and he didn't smile. "About that little birdie," he said. "What do you know about him?"

What?

"About Benji?"

Dom nodded and waited.

I suddenly felt scrutinised and defensive. "Uh . . ." I

shook my head. "That he's twenty-one years old. Been in his line of work for two years." I wasn't saying what that was out loud.

"Anything about his family?"

"Only that they weren't good people, and he spent his whole life dreaming of leaving them." I wasn't divulging that Benji had only told me this last night, but this was suddenly feeling like a formal line of questioning, and I wasn't divulging anything unless specifically asked.

"Do you know his last name?"

He wasn't going to like this.

"He told me it was Smith, but I highly doubt that's true." When Dom's eyes narrowed at me, I narrowed mine right back at him. "Hardly surprising to give actual names in his line of work, is it?" This was bullshit. "What's going on, Dom? Why the questions?"

He put the manila folder on my desk, atop the others. "I thought I recognised him, but I couldn't be sure," Dom said. "It took me a while to place him. He's older, thinned out a lot, but his eyes . . ."

I opened the folder.

File name Benecio Barbieri.

Son of Bruno and Emilia, deceased. Younger brother to Tommaso.

Current whereabouts unknown.

The black and white photograph was of a boy, maybe twelve. He was wearing a black suit, standing at a graveside funeral. He was shorter, had that pre-puberty chubbiness that told me he was about to shoot up two feet in two years. His curly hair was the same.

But his eyes.

"Jesus Christ."

The photo . . . His mother's funeral. Yet he stood apart from his father and brother. Alone. Twelve years old and alone at his own mother's funeral.

"I'm sorry," Dom said.

I looked up at him then. "What for?"

His gaze went to the folder. "It's . . . it's Benji."

I nodded. Because it was.

"He's been off radar for years," Dom added. "Went to boarding school, apparently, and never went home. Not during school holidays, not when he graduated. He just . . . disappeared."

"He said he grew up wanting nothing else but to leave them," I whispered.

"The cops don't know where he is," Dom said. "Couldn't find him. When Bruno Barbieri's case got blown wide open, he was questioned about everything, including the whereabouts of his youngest son. No one had seen him in years and at first, they speculated if Bruno had offed him. You know they'd always questioned whether he'd killed his wife . . ."

My head was starting to spin.

"But Bruno had laughed and said Benecio was . . . a string of homophobic words I won't repeat, and that he wouldn't have wasted a bullet."

I closed my eyes. Rage burned behind my ribs and just under my skin, blistering and burning so hot I couldn't form words. Hell, my only concerns were for Benji.

"I need to go home," I said, about to stand up.

"Nolan," Dom said. "This is . . . this is not good."

"No. He's at home by himself. I should be with him. Or something. I don't know."

"You're implicated," he said flatly. "This case is now in jeopardy. Every file, anything you've touched, which is all of it."

I stared at him, mouth open.

I hadn't even thought of that.

"No," I whispered, shaking my head. "No . . ."

He leaned in, his voice a whisper. "He's the son of Bruno Barbieri. The man we're trying to put away for some very serious crimes. The son, who is currently living at your house, and you're paying him for sexual—"

"No. I'm paying him for loss of income when I hit him with . . ."

"With your car," he finished for me. "Can you see how this looks?"

"He ran out in front of me," I countered. "He was being chased . . ."

Then I realised why he'd been running, blood draining from my face. "Oh fuck."

Dom was immediately concerned. "What is it? He was being chased?"

I nodded. "Who did you tell about this?"

"No one. I wanted to speak to you first."

I stood up and grabbed my jacket. "Come with me."

"Where are we going?"

"To speak to Benji."

Dom stood up but raised a hand. "Wait. I can't. I can't see him now that I know. I'm lead counsel—"

"You said his father wouldn't have bothered killing him because he's gay," I said, grabbing my keys and phone.

"Right."

"But he's been trying to find him, sending men to find him and chase him. He's staying at my place to lie low from the two men who were chasing him the night I hit him."

"What are you saying?"

"So Bruno wouldn't kill him for being gay," I said. "But maybe he would kill him for being a witness."

Dom scooped up the photos and folder. "Witness to what?"

"That's what we need to find out."

I WAS SO FREAKING NERVOUS. Equal measures of dread and fear made for a fast and possibly reckless drive home, but I pulled into my parking spot and Dom had to run to catch up to me. The stupid elevator took its miserable time, and for a second, I considered taking the stairs, until Dom clapped my back.

"Hey," he said. "Take a breath for me. And a second to think."

"Think about what?"

"About how this is bigger than just you and him, okay? There's a lot at stake here."

I glared at him as the elevator doors opened, and maybe that one second of grace stopped me from saying something I'd later regret.

We stepped inside and I thumped my floor number. "I'm very aware of that," I said, voice cool.

Dom grabbed my arm before the elevator stopped. "Look, Nolan. I don't know what's going on between you two, but your priorities—"

"My priorities?" I snapped at him. My priorities should have been the legal case. My priorities should have been ensuring Bruno Barbieri was put away for a long time. That was what we'd been working so hard for the past year for.

But they weren't. My priorities, in that moment, had never been clearer.

"He is my priority," I said.

The elevator doors opened and I raced to my front door.

"That's what I'm afraid of," Dom mumbled as he followed me.

Not waiting for him, I unlocked my door, leaving it open as I pushed in. "Benji?"

He was on the couch, book in hand, and relief slammed into me as soon as I saw him.

"Hey," he said, getting to his feet. "I wasn't expecting you. Is everything—"

I collected him in a hug. "Thank god you're okay."

"What's wrong?" he asked, and when I let go of him,

we both noticed Dom now standing inside, holding the manila folder.

Benji took a step back, his face paling, the book in his hand forgotten.

I grabbed his elbow. "It's okay, Benj. It's okay."

He shook his head, his wide eyes on me. The fear I saw in his eyes . . .

"It's okay," I whispered. "You're not in trouble."

"We need to talk though," Dom said. He walked over to the dining table, put the manila folder down, and took a seat.

I took the book from Benji, dumped it onto the couch, and slid my arm around his back. He was stiff and scared, so I pressed my lips to his forehead. "It'll be okay," I murmured. I rubbed his back for a second, then took his hand and led him to the table.

He came willingly, as if he was on autopilot.

Defeated.

I sat beside him, both of us opposite Dom, and kept our joined hands on Benji's thigh, my grip tight.

Dom opened the folder. The file name—Benji's real name—and the photograph of his mother's funeral on top.

Benji looked at them, then looked up, motionless. His face a mask of blank sadness.

"You know we're lawyers for the ODPP, I assume," Dom said. He was using his courtroom voice. Confident, stern, abrasive. I'd always admired the way he controlled the narrative, but I didn't like it as much now.

Benji didn't answer. He didn't move. Didn't even blink.

"Then you should know the case we're currently working on is the state against Bruno Barbieri."

Benji slow blinked, and I squeezed his hand. "I didn't know," I whispered. "Benji, I didn't know."

He still wouldn't look at me.

"You went off the grid," Dom continued. "Never accessed your bank accounts, phone, or contacted friends or family."

"Of course he didn't," I answered for him. "His family was the reason he left."

Dom's gaze cut to me in that unimpressed-lawyer way he did best. "The police had reason to believe he's dead, Nolan. Missing person, at least."

"Did he ever report me as missing?" Benji asked, his voice quiet and detached. "Did anyone?"

No. They hadn't. None of them had.

Even Dom didn't need to answer that.

"The men chasing you," Dom said, changing approach. "Are they your father's men?"

Benji took a few seconds to answer. I didn't think he was going to say anything at all, but he let out a quiet sigh. "Yes."

"Why?" Dom asked. "Is he just tying up loose ends? Or did you see something you shouldn't have? Do you know things you shouldn't?"

Benji looked at me then, a storm of emotions raging in his eyes before he stood up and tried to pull his hand from mine. "I need to go," he mumbled.

I stood up, and when he got his hand free from mine, I grabbed his arm instead. "Benji, please. You're safe here. He can't find you here. No one knows you're here."

He shot Dom a filthy glare. "Yes, they do. You do. *He* does." He tried to yank his arm away from me. "You wanna hand me back to him—"

"No!" I cried, holding onto him. "No. Never. I wouldn't allow it."

"Nolan," Dom murmured.

I spun to Dom. "Absolutely fucking not. I will declare involvement and this will be a mistrial before it even begins."

"I don't want to hand him over," Dom snapped. "Jesus Christ, Nolan. But this is already complicated enough. We cannot jeopardise this trial. You have a conflict of interest—"

"Fuck the case," I replied. "Fuck it all. I'm off the detail anyway, effective immediately."

"No," Benji said, still trying to get free. "Nolan, please let go of me."

I hadn't even been aware I was still holding onto him. I released my grip and he stood there, his chest heaving. "You don't know who you're dealing with. Whatever you think, however bad you think he is, it isn't even half of what he's done. The shit you have on him—whatever it is —won't matter." He shook his head. "He'll get off. He always does. He gets away with whatever the fuck he wants. You think him being in prison awaiting trial is stopping any of his business deals?" Benji laughed. "He's never been richer, more powerful. And my brother . . ."

He put his hand to his forehead, pale and on the verge of tears.

"Benji," I tried.

He shook his head and his eyes met mine. "I can't stay here. I can't put you in danger." He took a step back. "I'm sorry. I need to go."

"You're safe here," I tried.

"I'm not safe anywhere."

"What did you see?" Dom asked as he stood up. "What do you have on him? Your brother. Where is he in all of this?"

Benji took another step back from him, scared, and that just pissed me off.

"Enough, Dominic. Jesus fucking Christ."

"We can't help him if he doesn't tell us," Dom snapped.

"You cannot threaten him," I hissed.

Dom sighed. "I'm not. That's not what I meant."

Benji slipped behind me and went down the hall into my room. I shook my head at Dom. "This was not the plan."

Not that we really had a plan.

Maybe Dom's plan was to question Benji, but my plan was to make sure he was okay.

"What exactly are you trying to save here?" Dom asked. "I thought you were here for the case."

I pointed to the photo on the table. The one of the twelve-year-old boy crying alone at his mother's funeral. "This boy right here. That's who I'm here for. The one whose own father wants him dead. Who is on the run because his arsehole father, the man we're trying to put in prison, is trying to track him down." Then I pointed at Dom. "I will not let you or anyone else hurt him, do you under-fucking-stand?"

I left Dom standing there and went down to my room. Benji was standing at my bed, shoving the last of his shirts into his backpack.

"No, Benji, no," I whispered, going to him, trying to take his things out as he was trying to shove them in. "You can't go. Don't leave. You're safe here. We'll figure something out."

"You're in danger if I stay," he said, pulling the backpack away from me. "Your case, your work, your job." He shook his head. "I can't bring this shit down on you if I'm not here."

I shook my head, panic starting to kick in. "No. It's fine. I'm off the case. It's no big deal. There are a thousand other cases. This isn't your fault."

"Fitch and Ky," he said, tears welling in his eyes. "I put them in danger too. Everyone I care for. All I do is bring trouble, no matter where I go. I'm sorry." He sniffled, and the first tear escaped down his cheek. He tried to scrub it away, but I pulled him into my arms.

He had no fight in him anymore. He let me hold him and he sobbed.

"No, baby," I whispered. "You're no trouble. You did nothing wrong. You couldn't have known. Like I couldn't have known."

"If I'd told you my name . . ."

"If you'd told people your name, your father would

have found you a long time ago. You did what you needed to do. I would never question that."

He cried some more and I held him tighter. "It'll be okay, Benji. I promise. But I can't protect you if you leave. I know you're scared. I am too. But you'll be okay. Just stay until we figure something out. Please. Then—" I shrugged. "—if you still feel unsafe and want to go somewhere else, I'll drive you myself. Anywhere you want to go."

He sobbed, his whole body shaking. "Why are you so nice to me? Why are you doing this?"

I pulled back and cupped his face, making him look at me. He had tears streaming down his face, his dark lashes wet, eyes red. "Because you're worth it," I whispered. "You deserve to be looked after, shown the love you never had."

He recoiled a little and I realised I'd said the *L* word.

I hadn't exactly meant it like that, but he did deserve love. He deserved to be loved, to bask in it, to grow in it.

And if he stayed with me, I believed I could do that. I could love him so easily.

He heaved out a sob, barely able to speak. "I don't deserve love."

I pulled him back into my arms, holding him so damn tight. "You do. You do deserve love. To be loved, to know what it means to be loved so completely. You do, Benji. And if you give me a chance, I could be that person for you. If you let me."

He cried and cried, and I kept my arms around him until he cried himself out. I needed him to know that I wasn't going anywhere. After a while, he pulled back, wiping his eyes and nose, his face a blotchy, beautiful mess.

I wiped my thumb across his cheek and kissed his forehead. "You'll be okay. We'll make this right."

He frowned again, but he nodded. "I . . . I don't know how."

The truth was, I wasn't entirely sure either. "We'll work it out together. But he can't hurt you when you're here with me. I won't let it happen."

His gaze met mine. He looked so tired. As if he finally allowed himself to feel the weight of the last few years. He nodded, fresh tears welling in his eyes. "I don't know why you're so good to me."

Oh, this boy . . .

I pulled him in under my arm and kissed his forehead. "Then I'll just have to show you until you get it."

He froze. "Show me what?"

"That you're worth it," I said, trying to keep my tone nonchalant. "Come on, we better go see if Dominic's gone." I assumed he was because we'd been in my room a while. I'd have some fallout to deal with, I was certain of that much. But I didn't care. I was doing the right thing.

I'd always had a moral compass for right and wrong, and this was the right thing to do.

My career be damned.

I took Benji's hand and walked him out to the living room. I hadn't expected Dom to still be there, but he was. Standing at the glass door to the balcony, looking out at the world, his hands clasped behind his back.

"Oh," I said, surprised.

He glanced over his shoulder and sighed before turning around to face us. "I'm surprised to still be here too," he said flatly, just as the intercom buzzed.

My gaze went to the door, and I pulled Benji behind me.

"I called someone," Dom explained as he walked over and let whoever the hell it was into my apartment complex.

"What the hell?" I asked, incredulous. "Who? Who did you call, Dominic?"

Who the fuck did he think he was?

"What have you done?"

He sighed again and opened my front door. I had no clue who was about to walk in. Cops? The DA? Our boss?

But they didn't walk in. They ran and skidded to a stop in my living room.

Fitch.

And a taller guy followed a second later.

Dominic had called Fitch?

Fitch saw no one but Benji. He bypassed me and collected him in a fierce hug. The second guy, whom I wasn't sure I knew, came over and ruffled Benji's hair.

Dominic closed the door and met my stunned gaze. "We need to talk."

TEN
BENJI

I WAS SO OVERWHELMED. By everything, by everyone.

I'd gone from having the best morning to having it all upended in a second. And, I realised, as Dominic sat opposite me with that goddamn file with those photos and my real name, the worst part wasn't knowing I'd been found out.

It was knowing I had to leave Nolan.

That he knew I'd lied to him. That I'd hurt him.

That my time with him was over, ending in the worst possible way.

That was worse than anything my father could threaten me with. Worse than what my father's henchmen could ever do to me if they'd caught me.

The way he sat on my side of the table, holding my hand, only made it worse.

The legal case he'd been working on had been the one against my father.

The odds of that were astronomical. The odds of him forgiving me even worse.

Packing my bag and leaving was the only thing I could think of doing. Getting out of there, running away, going into hiding all over again was the only choice I had.

Until Nolan begged me not to go. Until he held me and told me I was worth fighting for.

I'd never needed to hear anything more in my life.

He was a rescue boat when I was drowning in a sea of fear and guilt.

My god, the way he'd held me. Mending something in me that he didn't break. Healing wounds he didn't inflict.

I clung to that hope like I clung to him.

I didn't understand why he was doing it. He'd said it was because I was worth it, and while I didn't believe that, he promised to prove it.

And he promised to show me what love meant, if I'd let him.

Love.

Actual love.

If I could ever love anyone, it would be Nolan.

How he'd put himself between me and Dominic when the door intercom buzzed . . .

When he said he'd protect me, he meant it.

But then Fitch and Ky were there, and I was crying again.

Dominic had called Fitch?

I couldn't get my head around that. Around anything.

"Benji," Nolan murmured. "I need to speak to Dominic. Would you please give us a moment?"

I wasn't sure where we could go in his one-bedroom apartment aside from the one bedroom, so that was where I took them.

I closed the door behind them, and they stood there, watching me. "The fuck happened?" Fitch said. "Are you okay? You've been crying, Benj. I ain't ever seen you cry before."

I went to the bed, pulled back the covers, and crawled into the middle of the bed. I patted either side of me. "I'm tired."

They both toed out of their sneakers and Fitch dove into the closest side, Ky crawling over me, and they both encased me, cuddling me. Fitch pulled the covers up and grabbed the remote control, pressing the TV on.

"This is amazing," he said.

Ky noticed my backpack still at the foot of the bed. "Are you leaving?"

I sighed. "I tried, but Nolan wants me to stay. He . . . said he can look after me if I stay. Protect me."

"He looked a bit protective when we got here," Fitch said. "Standing in front of you like that. It was hot."

I snorted, because of course he'd think it was hot. I would have normally cracked a joke about that, but I wasn't feeling it. "He . . . said he could show me what it means to be loved if I'd let him."

They both froze, then popped their heads up to look at me. It was almost funny, but all I could do was cry again. "He's so fucking nice. I don't know what I ever did to deserve him."

"You got hit by his car," Ky said.

"You let him come inside you," Fitch said.

Ky swatted Fitch's arm but it did make me laugh.

"What?" he cried. "It's true. I told you!"

Ky sighed. "Well, it's not *un*true."

I let out a shaky breath. "He's on the legal team in my father's trial. It's a mess. Him even knowing me could jeopardise the whole case. Let alone a personal relationship. He could lose his job, probably. I don't know. It's so unfair. Because he didn't know. I never told him my real name."

"That's right," Fitch said. "So it's not your fault. It's not his fault either."

"But he knows it now," I mumbled. "And if he doesn't admit it, report it or whatever, then he's in trouble. He said something about a possible mistrial. Fucking hell, what if my father walks free because of me?"

Fitch held me a little tighter. "Then we need to make sure that doesn't happen." Then he added, "Dom will make sure it doesn't happen. He's a legal wizard or something."

"He called you?" I asked. "When he said he'd called someone, I was expecting cops, not gonna lie."

"Yes," Fitch said with a wiggle. "Thought he was putting in a booty call and I got all excited, like hell fucking yes, I'm up for a lunch-break fuck. Then he told me you were in trouble and you needed me, so here we are."

"Sorry you missed your booty call," I said.

He sighed dramatically. "I'll forgive you this one time."

"I have to say," I whispered, "when Dominic was sitting across from me with the case file of me, he was kinda scary."

"Mmm," Fitch said, wiggling again. "Did he use his big bad daddy voice? Because it's fucking hot."

Ky laughed this time and I gave Fitch a nudge. "I said he scared me. But then he called you, so I'm not sure what to make of him."

Fitch sighed. "Lemme tell you something about that man. He ain't nothing but a big old teddy bear. Hard and cold on the outside, soft and gooey in the middle."

"Like all good daddies should be," Ky added.

"You two are fucking perverts," I mumbled. "I love you both."

We were quiet for a moment, watching some millionaire real estate show on the TV. My eyes were getting heavier and these two warm bodies snuggling into me were making me drowsy.

The emotional onslaught from before had taken it out of me.

"I think you should fight him," Fitch said quietly.

I blinked myself awake. "Fight who?"

"Your father."

I shook my head. My immediate response was no. Like a reflex. Don't fight back because he wins every time, and the resulting punishment is never worth it. It was ingrained in me to never fight back, to never question.

"Think about it," Fitch said. "Now's the only chance you'll probably ever get. He's already in prison, awaiting his trial. He can't come for you. He can send whoever he wants in his place, but it's not him. You don't have to face him." Then he shrugged. "And you've got two lawyers on your side who are out there right now, probably trying to figure out how to beat him while protecting you. There's never been a better chance, Benj. Think of it like the boss fight at the end of a video game but you don't have to fight him alone. You get to join forces with other fighters to bring him down."

Was . . . was that . . . could that be true?

I . . . I wasn't sure.

"I think he's right," Ky said. "When are you ever gonna have the state's best lawyers on your side?"

"I don't know," I whispered. "If he knows I helped them, he'll never stop coming for me. The best I can do is hope they put him away for a while and he has so much other shit going on that he forgets about me."

"That's not gonna happen," Fitch murmured. "You know things he doesn't want people to know."

I sighed.

I knew what they were saying was right. This was the best chance I ever had. The only chance I'd ever get for any hope of being free from the dark shadow that was my father.

But fear was stopping me. Valid fear, fear taught to

me by firsthand experience of just what my father was capable of.

I wasn't strong enough.

"Can you give an anonymous tip?" Ky asked.

Fitch snorted. "Hmm, love me some anonymous tip."

Ky reached over and gave him a hard shove. "Do you ever not think about sex, whore?"

Fitch laughed and even I managed a smile just as there was a quiet knock on the door. Then it opened and Nolan stuck his head in, but he did a double take when he saw the three of us in bed.

"Oh."

Then the door opened wider and Dominic was there.

"I was going to ask if everything was okay," Nolan said, smiling at me. "But I can see it is."

"We are, unfortunately, fully dressed," Fitch said, throwing back the covers as proof. "But if Dominic thinks I've been naughty, I'll take the punishment."

Ky and I both shoved Fitch again, and though I couldn't be sure, Dominic might have smirked. Right before he scowled, that was.

Nolan, on the other hand, gave me a warm, gentle smile. "Got a second?"

"Of course," I said, sitting up. I needed Fitch to get out of bed first, which he did, and Ky followed, so the three of us went out to the living room.

Nolan slipped his hand in mine, and I sat next to him on the sofa. Dom took the single-seater, Ky sat next to me and Fitch sat on the arm rest.

Nolan threaded our fingers and covered our hands

with his other. An absolute pillar of strength, of kindness. Of all that was good in this world. "Okay, so between us, we think we've come up with a plan," he said.

"Wait," I said, my voice quiet. "Before you say anything. Before you do anything, like quit or recuse yourself or whatever you said before." I took a deep breath in, not sure if I had the strength to do this. But god, what Fitch said before was right. I'd never get another chance. I'd never be stronger than I was with these two lawyers helping me.

With Nolan holding my hand.

"I want to help."

"Help with what?" Nolan asked.

"Taking my father down. Putting an end to it all. I can't live looking over my shoulder anymore. I keep putting Fitch and Ky in danger, and now you, Nolan. I can't have you losing your job for me. I won't." I met his gaze, his soft, beautiful eyes. "You're too important to me."

"Benji, baby, you don't have to do anything you don't want," he whispered.

"I want to do this. What Fitch said is right." I gave Fitch a smile then. "I'll never have a better chance than now. So, while I didn't think I'd ever be ready to do this, now it is."

Dominic leaned forward, his eyes narrowing at me. "Are you certain?"

I managed a nod. "Yes." Then I swallowed hard and found the courage to say the next part out loud. "You know about the drug money and the weapon imports."

That was nothing new; they'd been trying to pin his crimes on him for years. How they were going to provide evidence that he was the mastermind behind it all was the point of the whole case. "But you wanted to know what I saw, what I knew, what I witnessed."

Nolan squeezed my hand.

Dominic nodded. "Yes."

"He killed my mother."

Every set of eyes were on me, wide, their faces pale. Nolan exhaled a ragged breath. "Oh my god."

My hands trembled, my whole body strung tight. "And I have proof."

ELEVEN
NOLAN

WHEN BENJI GOT up from the couch and went to my room, the four of us sat there in silence. From Fitch's expression, I was sure not even he knew about this. The weight of what Benji had just said hung over us like a dark and heavy cloud.

A weight that Benji had carried on his own for far too long.

I met Dominic's gaze, his expression grim. Whatever proof Benji was about to provide could be huge. It could also be completely inadmissible. But for me, it changed nothing.

My priority was Benji.

The reason why I would gladly step back from this case, possibly from my career, all for a man I'd known for less than one week, was something I'd have to explain to Dominic later.

Though I'm sure it was obvious, but I owed that to him.

He'd been my mentor, my friend, for many years. I owed him the truth.

I cared for Benji.

Deeply. And if Benji decided, when all this was said and done, that he didn't want to continue seeing me, I still wouldn't regret standing up for him.

That was how I knew I was doing the right thing.

Because it was a principle thing.

Helping Benji, protecting him, was the right thing to do.

Benji came back out with an old hand-held video game console. The kind that flipped open with a small grey screen. Not what I'd been expecting at all.

He sat back down next to me, turning it over in his hand. "It's a Nintendo DS. I got it when I was about five," he said quietly. "They're mostly for games, but they can also record stuff. About a year after my mother died, I was using it to make videos. There was a trend going around to use your old DS like it was some vintage camera." He took a deep breath in and Fitch slid off the armrest and squeezed himself next to Benji, putting his arms around him.

Then Benji flipped the DS open and turned it on.

"I didn't mean to record my father's conversation. I wasn't supposed to hear it. I have no idea if he knows I heard it, but I suspect he does. I never believed my mother overdosed. Not for a second. She was excited about taking me to the state theatre on the weekend. She'd bought tickets. Just us two. It was always just us two. My brother was my father's favourite, being the eldest son and all. My father hated that I was more like my mother. He blamed her for me not being into all the typical boy things. But my mum would never have left me alone with them. I know that in my heart."

Jesus Christ, I hated that man.

Benji pressed some buttons on the game console. "Anyway, I recorded this by accident. I never knew what to do with it. I wanted to take it to the police, but he'd boasted before about how he had some cops on his payroll, so I never knew who to trust."

My gaze cut to Dominic's and his to mine.

This was news to us.

Benji put the DS on the coffee table and pressed play. "The first part is just me . . ."

And there on that tiny grey screen was a young Benji. He was filming himself, like a selfie; his young face and curly hair filled the small screen. He was walking inside what looked like a large, lavish house. Tall ceilings, a chandelier, art on the walls. He was talking about his shirt, of all things. It was new and expensive, and it was a typical video of a kid that age.

But then there was the sound of a door slamming and the young Benji froze, the screen going dark but the audio was still on.

"Father," young Benji said quietly.

"Benecio," his father snapped. "Can't you see I'm on the phone?"

"Sorry," young Benji squeaked, and my heart hurt.

I took his hand again, holding it tight.

There was a muffled sound, presumably Benji walking, then after a moment, his father's voice again. It was muted, as if Benji was standing outside the room. "He's a fucking traitor. I'll deal with him like I dealt with Luzon and my wife. No one betrays me. No one. If Arad thinks he can undercut me, I'll show him the cost of loyalty . . . No, not a suicide or a car accident. I'm not protecting any kids anymore. Tell Snake to take him out in front of his kids for all I care. I want this to send a message so people know not to fuck with me . . ."

In the audio, young Benji's breathing was louder, and I could just picture him, a scared-as-hell little boy clutching his game console to his chest.

Bruno's voice sounded closer now. "Fine. Payment when it's done. I want to see it on the evening news . . ."

Then younger Benji was panting, running, and the recording ended soon after.

Benji reached over and closed the Nintendo. "He's talking about my mother," he said. "He says like how I dealt with my wife, and he says making it look like a suicide. My mother never betrayed him. Maybe she wanted to leave him, I don't know. She was scared of him, same as me. He would never allow her to leave him. Not alive, anyway."

"Benji," I whispered. "I'm so sorry. You must have been petrified."

He looked at me then, his eyes full of sadness. "I left two weeks later for boarding school. I started year seven at Kings. I could have lived at home but my father wanted me out of the house." He managed a sad smile. "All the boys I went to school with hated boarding that first year. They all wanted to go home. They missed home. I was the happiest I'd been since before my mother died. I was finally free. I was out of that house, away from him. I never wanted to go back. And in the end, I didn't. When school finished, I moved out but didn't go home. It took my dad a week to notice." He nodded toward the DS on the coffee table. "I've kept this with me though, and I've kept it charged so the battery didn't die. I don't know why I kept it. I wanted to smash it a hundred times, just to delete what I knew. But something told me to keep it."

"I'm glad you did," I murmured, holding his hand in both of mine.

"Those names your father mentioned," Dominic said. "Luzon and Arad. They're both dead. Luzon was in a car accident. Ran off the road, other driver never found. It was treated as suspicious because of his ties to the crime syndicate and your father, but the case went cold. And Anthony Arad was gunned down in his own driveway, in front of his kids."

Benji nodded, his lips pressed together. "Yeah. Just like he said."

"And Snake," I added. "Jake 'the snake' Moreno."

Dominic nodded. "Definitely."

"Who's that?" Ky asked.

"Notorious bikie," I answered. "Has spent half his life in prison for violent crimes. Claims several murders, never been charged due to lack of evidence."

Dominic sighed, leaning forward, his elbows on his knees. "Benji, we're going to need to take your device," he said gently. "And we're going to need to speak to the police."

Benji stared at his lap, at our joined hands, and gave the smallest nod. "Will it do any good?" Another tear rolled down his cheek and he scrubbed it away. "Because my father will know where this recording came from. And those guys who've been trying to find me will be the least of my worries."

I let go of his hand so I could put my arm around him instead. I pulled him closer, which included Fitch as well. I didn't mind. Benji was going to need all the support he could get.

"We'll do everything we can to keep you out of it," Dom said gently. "There are procedures in place for cases like this. Protocols, security measures. And," he added with a bit of a smile, "hopefully with this new evidence, he'll never see the outside of a prison again."

"And my brother?" Benji asked. "He knows everything my father's done. The money, the murders. My father offloaded a bunch of shell company stuff in his name, and he's been running business matters for years. He's as complicit as my father. If you want to end the Barbieri family crime business—if you really want to keep me safe—you'll need to stop him too."

Dominic stared at him for a second and I knew what he was thinking because I was thinking it too. "They looked into your brother's companies," Dom said uncertainly.

I nodded. "Not entirely ethical, but nothing illegal."

"Look into Murzik and Raynor Pty Ltd," Benji said. "It's a real estate front in Vanuatu. Tax free property something or other. I don't really understand how it works, but it was my brother's idea. I remember him telling my father about it and my father was so proud. They discussed how to make it look on paper." Benji shrugged again. "I was only young when they talked about it, and I didn't understand it. All I know is dirty money goes in, clean money comes out."

Dominic's jaw ticked and he had fire in his eyes when he looked at me. I knew he wanted to smile. Hell, he probably wanted to laugh. Because this was pure gold. If we could prove any of what Benji had just told us, with the voice recording and fresh new investigations and charges, the Barbieri's were finished.

Dominic looked at Benji, dead serious now. "Benji, before I make some calls, I need to know if you're one hundred percent certain you want to do this."

Benji looked at him and barked out a teary laugh. "I'm scared shitless right now," he said, squeezing my hand. "But yes. I need this to end. And it will never end unless I do this."

I was both proud of him and scared for him.

Dominic stood up. "Good boy."

Fitch shot him a look. "Hey. None of that from you to him, mister. That's for me only."

And it was the perfect moment of levity we needed. Ky snorted and Benji chuckled, wiping his face. Dom huffed at Fitch, but there was a hint of humour in it.

And we all took a minute to breathe and collect our

thoughts. Dominic stood over by the dining table, putting in calls to some pretty important people.

I kept an ear on his one-sided conversations while I sat with Benji, rubbing his back. "You'll be okay," I told him. "You can stay here until we get everything sorted out. You'll be safe here. And I meant what I said before. If you don't want anything . . . you're not obligated to . . . you don't have to sleep in my bed is what I'm trying to say. Only if you want to. I would never—"

"I want to," Benji said quickly. "Nolan, I want to stay here with you." Then he swallowed hard and looked at Fitch and Ky. "I can't go back to the apartment right now," he said. "Sorry. But it's too exposed and I can't put you in danger. God, maybe you two shouldn't even stay there. I'll still cover my rent . . . somehow . . . until we know what's going on, at least."

"Hey," Fitch said softly. "It's okay. We'll be okay. As long as you're safe here. And I totally get it. He has the big apartment and the big bed and the big dick. I'd take it too. Actually," Fitch looked around Benji to me. "If you want another—"

Benji shoved him. "No."

I chuckled and kissed Benji's shoulder. "You'll be okay, Benji. I'm proud of you."

Benji shot me a look, eyes wide and still a little glassy. "You are?"

Oh, this poor sweet boy.

"Of course I am. I'm so proud of you. This isn't going to be easy. Some days it'll feel like a mountain you just can't climb. But you're doing the right thing. One step at a time. Just know, Benji, you're not alone."

Fitch gave him a squeeze. "You have us. And you have Mr Big Apartment with the Big Dick."

Dominic made a displeased sound. He was still on the phone, but he stalked over to Fitch and, holding Fitch's chin, put his finger to his lips. He mouthed the word *enough*.

Fitch moaned quietly, blushing like a schoolboy. He looked up at Dom, his eyelashes fluttering, and when Dominic made a low sound, Fitch squirmed.

Well, holy shit.

I couldn't even process that.

It was quite the sight to see. It felt as if I'd intruded on a private moment, and I was quick to look away.

But Ky made a purring sound. "I would one hundred percent watch that," he murmured. "Damn."

Dominic huffed and walked back to the dining table, and Fitch melted, fanning his face.

Benji chuckled, leaning into me, his head on my shoulder. These three boys sure were something else. I couldn't help but like them. But Benji . . . he was more than that.

He was something special.

And what Dominic had said to me when we were alone, when the boys were in my room, came back to me.

"I can see you have feelings for the boy," he'd said. "And he seems drawn to you."

"I need to protect him," I'd replied, not ready to name

what I actually felt for Benji. "I can't explain it. He's . . . special to me."

Dominic had held my gaze. "You'd really jeopardise your entire career for him."

I'd nodded. "I would. It's the right thing to do."

He'd sighed and stared out to the balcony for a long moment. "And what about his career?"

His job as a rent boy?

"I don't care," I'd replied. "You can't sit there and tell me it bothers you when you and Fitch are so well-acquainted. You have his number?"

His eyes met mine before he rolled his with a sigh. "You're welcome, by the way," he'd said. "For calling him instead of the police commissioners office."

Then it was my turn to sigh. "I need to help him. I can't ask you to jeopardise your career, but I'm not abandoning him."

Dominic did that hard stare thing that usually made courtroom witnesses crumble. But I knew this man, and I needed him to know how serious I was. "Are you ready to do this?" he'd asked. "Are you ready to take this step? Because there's no going back after this."

I'd looked him dead in the eye. "I'm ready."

And I was.

Sitting on the couch with Benji now, holding his hand, I knew I was ready.

I gave Benji another kiss on the side of the head. "Can I get you anything?" I asked him quietly.

Benji shook his head and snuggled in closer. He was

almost sitting on my lap, and I was half tempted to pull him onto me, but just then, Dominic ended his call.

"Okay," he said, coming to stand in front of us. He took a deep breath. "Here's what's going to happen."

A WEEK LATER, Dominic and I sat in my car on Oxford Street at ten o'clock at night, watching the three boys. They were talking, laughing, interacting with passers-by.

Flirting, playing it up. Being loud.

Being themselves.

Benji wore his black jeans that slung low enough to reveal his hip bones, and a pink Strawberry Shortcake crop top that looked hot as hell. His black curls shone under the neon lights, and I swear to god, I'd never seen anyone sexier than him right then.

A man approached them, aiming for Fitch, and the little punk flirted before he turned him down. Dominic growled, and I snorted. "He knows you're watching. He wants you to punish him later."

Dominic narrowed his eyes out the windscreen.

"You are seeing him later, yes?" I asked.

He cut me a dirty side-eye that told me yes, but also to shut up and mind my own business.

I smiled to myself, just as two men approached the boys. They trained in like sharks on Benji, making him take a step back. Then I saw what one of them was holding. My heart skidded to a stop. "He has a gun," I said, fumbling for the door handle.

"Wait," Dominic said, grabbing my arm.

Then Benji gave the sign. He put both his hands up, and in an instant, swarms of cops descended from the darkness and surrounded them. Fitch and Ky pulled Benji away, and after a two-second standoff, the two men were now face down on the ground, then Dominic let go of my arm. "Okay, let's go."

I was out of that car so fast and running across the street, crowds and traffic be damned. Benji was fine, I could see that, but he was searching for me, and he sagged when he saw me coming.

I collected him in a hug, holding him tight. "It's okay. It's over."

He nodded into my neck. Because it *was* over. Well, the two hired henchmen were done. Benji didn't have to worry about them anymore. And after a tense week—and years of stress for Benji—it seemed surreal for this to be over. Even though the real battle hadn't even begun yet.

Another piece of the giant Barbieri crime ring puzzle was sliding into place. There were a lot of pieces to go, but every step forward was a win. Benji had done more than enough, and now it was up to the police and legal team to do their parts.

I wouldn't be on that legal team, but I'd be beside Benji every step of the way.

I pulled back and took in Benji's face, his body. "Are you hurt?"

He shook his head. "No."

Dominic was with Fitch and Ky, and the cops were hauling the two men away.

"What do you need?" I asked Benji. "You name it."

"I just want to go home."

Home.

Sounded good to me. The police knew where to find us if they needed to.

I tucked Benji under my arm and turned to the others. "Are you guys okay? Benji wants to go home."

Fitch and Ky both nodded, and Fitch gave Benji's arm a squeeze. "I'll call you."

He gave them both a hug.

I met Dominic's eyes. "Do you need a lift?"

He inhaled deeply, his eyes darting to Fitch. "No, I'm good. I'll make sure this one gets home."

Fitch grinned, his tongue licking the side of his mouth.

"Ky, what about you?" I asked.

He started walking backwards, heading up toward the 180 club. He gave us a smile. "I'm all good, thanks. Talk to you tomorrow, Benj."

Benji nodded and he tightened his arm around me. "Nolan."

"Okay, sweetheart. Let's get you home."

He was exhausted.

The police operation to get the two men who'd chased Benji was now a weight off his shoulders.

Such a relief.

As soon as we were home, he kicked off his shoes, left his jeans on the floor, and crawled into bed, wearing nothing but his briefs and that damn crop top.

There was no sex that night, or the day that followed.

Benji simply needed comfort and strength in the form of warm embraces, gentle touches, and soft kisses. He needed support and solidarity.

I was more than happy to give it to him.

TWELVE
BENJI

WHEN NOLAN HAD SAID it wouldn't be easy, he wasn't kidding.

It started with police reports and interviews. But not with normal cops. These were some high-ranking badges, and as intimidating as it was, Nolan was with me the whole time.

And Dominic.

I had a newfound respect for Dominic. He was a hard-arse, but he took no bullshit and he protected me from the wrong kind of questions, helping me understand when and what to answer.

Nolan just protected me from everything else.

He held my hand the entire time, and he was my shield against the curious looks and whispers. He even reminded one lady—who decided to question the legality and moral integrity of my job—that I was on their side, there to help *them* despite the obvious threat to my own life.

I loved that Nolan had defended me, ripping into her like he did. I'd expected Dominic to tell Nolan to be quiet, but he didn't. He stared at the woman until she apologised to me.

And I knew then that what Fitch had said before was true. I would never be this protected, never be this prepared to take on my father than I would be with these guys on my team.

Now that I was no longer in hiding, I cleaned out my old bank account. That money had sat untouched for years, and it seemed surreal to call it mine now, after all those times in the last few years I'd been lucky to scrape together a few bucks.

I also had my Medicare card back and my school certificates, which meant maybe I could truly begin to think about my future.

My *actual* future.

After all the police interviews and after I'd handed over the evidence, all the names and details, we could do nothing but wait.

It was going to take time, Nolan explained, to make sure everything was done to the absolute letter of the law.

He was taken off my father's case.

He said it was fine. It was procedure and protocol, and he wouldn't do anything to jeopardise the rest of the trial. He'd said his department wasn't even mad because the new evidence was, as they'd said, hopefully, the metaphorical nail in the coffin of my father's freedom.

And possibly my brother's.

While I hated that Nolan's work was affected, that

he'd had to hand over all the work he'd done in the last year, I was also kinda glad.

I didn't want him involved.

I didn't want his name to ever come across my father's ears.

Then came the discussions about my safety and the likelihood of changing my name. I wasn't sure about that.

I hadn't been Benecio Barbieri for a long time. I also hadn't any documentation, which had proved difficult these last few years. No Medicare card meant no hospitals or doctor appointments. Not having access to a bank account meant living cash-only. No proof of who I was.

That I even existed.

But I had those back now. I had myself back now.

Even if I was to become someone else.

But, like I'd told Nolan when we were eating dinner four days later, changing my name won't stop my father from finding me.

"So do it anyway," he'd said. "Take back some control. Don't let your father's name be a dark cloud hanging over you."

"What name would I choose?"

"You told me your name was Benji Smith. That's a good a name as any."

"Or," I hedged, "I could call myself Benji O'Brien."

Nolan dropped his fork.

It made me laugh. "You own me anyway, so it'd just be making it easier."

He cleared his throat, cheeks pink. "I don't *own* you."

I snorted and leaned in closer. "You *own* me in every

sense of the word, Nolan. I belong to you. I have your DNA in me, and that makes me yours." I wiggled in my seat to remind him of how exactly he'd put his DNA in me. "I'm pretty sure that's how it works."

He made a face, embarrassed. "I don't think that's how it works at all." He pushed his plate away. "But thanks for the visual."

I chuckled, but my smile faded. "That wasn't a no," I said. "It also wasn't a yes."

"About what? Changing your surname to match mine?" His eyes met mine. "Were you serious?"

I nodded. "I was, yes. But if you don't want me to, I won't. I'll pick something else. What's Dominic's surname again? Maybe he'll adopt me."

Nolan growled at me. "No." Then he moved his seat out so he could face me properly. He took my hands. "Benji, baby, listen. If you want to change your name to O'Brien, I can't stop you. I wouldn't stop you."

I pouted. "But? There's a but coming, isn't there?"

He narrowed his brows and touched his thumb to my lips. "No pouting."

I sighed instead.

"But," he began, "if you wanted to wait, we could possibly, maybe"—he cringed—"change your name the old-fashioned way."

I laughed . . . until I realised he was serious. Then I gawped at him. "The old-fashioned way . . . Nolan. Are you . . . is that . . . what the fuck?"

He chuckled. "It's too early right now, I know that. But you need to know where I stand with you. I could so easily spend forever with you. I mean that. The way I feel, the way you make me feel . . . I'm falling in love with you, Benji."

Holy fucking shit.

"So, if there's no immediate rush to change your name, then maybe when the time is right, you can have my surname."

Emotions I'd been trying to keep in check, the need to be loved and accepted, surged to the surface and I began to cry.

He, of course, looked horrified. He pulled me onto his lap. "No, Benji, it's okay. It's fine. If you want to change your name now, that's fine too. Hell, I'd love you to have my name. Fucking hell yes, I would. Not that it would mean I own you but—"

"Yes, you would," I said, still crying, wiping my nose. "You do already. I'm yours, Nolan. Surname or not. And you're falling in love with me," I said, crying harder. "I can't believe that. Why? I mean, god, Nolan. I'm a mess. My life is a mess. My father's a piece of shit, I'm a hooker. And you love me? What's wrong with you?"

He laughed, pulling me in for a kiss. "I don't care about any of that. I just care about you. The past is past. I'm more interested in your future. And mine. Together." He wiped my face and studied my eyes. "Whatever you decide to do, whatever you want. I'll support you. If you want to go back to work with Fitch and Ky, then that's okay with me."

"What?"

What the hell?

"If you decide you want to keep working," he said with a shrug. "I'd maybe have to put down some rules. Like protected sex only. No kissing. That kind of thing."

I couldn't believe what he was saying.

"No." I was almost offended. "No one touches me but you. No one. I can't even think about another man touching me. Why would you want that?"

"I don't want that. I thought you wanted that." He shook his head, his eyes imploring. "I would never change you or stop you from being who you are. You once said that you loved your job, so if you wanted to keep working—"

I put my forehead to his, crying again. Unable to stop the tears. He was just so understanding, so nice. So perfect. "I don't know what I'll do. I have some money now and I'll figure something out, but I can't go back to that. I don't want anyone else to touch me. I don't want to touch anyone but you. I love sex, yes. But Nolan, baby, only with you. You're all I need." I kissed him. "I love you," I whispered. "I love how you love me. I can't ask for anything more." Then I pouted. "Except maybe your surname."

He laughed, cupping my face and bringing me in for another warm, soft kiss. "Then consider it yours."

I hugged him and laughed, despite the tears. "I love you, Nolan O'Brien," I said again.

"And I love you, Benji . . ." He paused, his eyes scanning mine. "Benji O'Brien."

I laughed, so ridiculously happy and so, so very loved. "We should celebrate, and I know just the thing."

He snorted. "What's that?"

"Me. In my Strawberry Shortcake crop top and not much else. Don't think I didn't realise how much you liked me in it."

He laughed, his smile fading into something serene as he studied my face. "I'm gonna celebrate the hell out of you. For as long as you'll let me."

"Are you talking about tonight? Or waaaay into the future? Because I plan on letting you celebrate me forever, Nolan. No one could ever make me happier."

He kissed me sweetly. "Forever."

I was so freaking happy. I booped my finger on the tip of his nose. "You know what would make me happier though?"

"Hmm," he hummed. "What's that?"

"If I was face down on your bed right now, wearing nothing but that crop top, and—"

He stood up, carrying me and making me laugh, and walked us to his bedroom. Oh, I wore the crop top all right, and nothing else.

And he celebrated me for hours.

Reminding me over and over that no matter what the future brought our way, we'd be okay.

I'd be okay.

I was stronger now and safe.

And loved.

And that was the only future I needed.

The end

FITCH, BOOK TWO

Preorder Fitch now!

Amazon

KYLAN, BOOK THREE

Preorder Kylan now!

Amazon

ABOUT THE AUTHOR

N.R. Walker is an Australian author who loves her genre of queer romance. First published in 2012, she now has over 70 books, many which are also audiobooks, and numerous translations done in nine different languages.

She loves writing and spends far too much time doing it but wouldn't have it any other way.

---

nrwalker.net

ALSO BY N.R. WALKER

Blind Faith

Through These Eyes (Blind Faith #2)

Blindside: Mark's Story (Blind Faith #3)

Ten in the Bin

Gay Sex Club Stories 1

Gay Sex Club Stories 2

Gay Sex Club Stories 3

Point of No Return – Turning Point #1

Breaking Point – Turning Point #2

Starting Point – Turning Point #3

Element of Retrofit – Thomas Elkin Series #1

Clarity of Lines – Thomas Elkin Series #2

Sense of Place – Thomas Elkin Series #3

Taxes and TARDIS

Three's Company

Red Dirt Heart

Red Dirt Heart 2

Red Dirt Heart 3

Red Dirt Heart 4

Red Dirt Christmas

Cronin's Key

Cronin's Key II

Cronin's Key III

Cronin's Key IV - Kennard's Story

Exchange of Hearts

The Spencer Cohen Series, Book One

The Spencer Cohen Series, Book Two

The Spencer Cohen Series, Book Three

The Spencer Cohen Series, Yanni's Story

Blood & Milk

The Weight Of It All

A Very Henry Christmas (The Weight of It All 1.5)

Perfect Catch

Switched

Imago

Imagines

Imagoes

Red Dirt Heart Imago

On Davis Row

Finders Keepers

Evolved

Galaxies and Oceans

Private Charter

Nova Praetorian

A Soldier's Wish

Upside Down

The Hate You Drink

Sir

Tallowwood

Reindeer Games

The Dichotomy of Angels

Throwing Hearts

Pieces of You - Missing Pieces #1

Pieces of Me - Missing Pieces #2

Pieces of Us - Missing Pieces #3

Lacuna

Tic-Tac-Mistletoe

Bossy

Code Red

Dearest Milton James

Dearest Malachi Keogh

Christmas Wish List

Code Blue

Davo

The Kite

Learning Curve

Merry Christmas Cupid

To the Moon and Back

Second Chance at First Love

Outrun the Rain

Into the Tempest

Touch the Lightning

EWB - Enemies With Benefits

Holiday Heart Strings

Bloom

The Men from Echo Creek

Method Acting

The Bait

Nothing Left to Lose

Deck the Fire Halls

TITLES IN AUDIO:

Cronin's Key

Cronin's Key II

Cronin's Key III

Red Dirt Heart

Red Dirt Heart 2

Red Dirt Heart 3

Red Dirt Heart 4

The Weight Of It All

Switched

Point of No Return

Breaking Point

Starting Point

Spencer Cohen Book One

Spencer Cohen Book Two

Spencer Cohen Book Three

Yanni's Story

On Davis Row

Evolved

Elements of Retrofit

Clarity of Lines

Sense of Place

Blind Faith

Through These Eyes

Blindside

Finders Keepers

Galaxies and Oceans

Nova Praetorian

Upside Down

Sir

Tallowwood

Imago

Throwing Hearts

Sixty Five Hours

Taxes and TARDIS

The Dichotomy of Angels

The Hate You Drink

Pieces of You

Pieces of Me

Pieces of Us

Tic-Tac-Mistletoe

Lacuna

Bossy

Code Red

Learning to Feel

Dearest Milton James

Dearest Malachi Keogh

Three's Company

Christmas Wish List

Code Blue

Davo

The Kite

Learning Curve

Merry Christmas Cupid

To the Moon and Back

Second Chance at First Love

Outrun the Rain

Into the Tempest

Touch the Lightning

EWB

Holiday Heart Strings

Bloom

The Men from Echo Creek

Method Acting

The Bait

Deck the Fire Halls

SERIES COLLECTIONS:

Red Dirt Heart Series

Turning Point Series

Thomas Elkin Series

Spencer Cohen Series

Imago Series

Blind Faith Series

Missing Pieces Series

The Storm Boys Series

Gay Sex Club Stories

FREE READS:

Sixty Five Hours

Learning to Feel

His Grandfather's Watch (And The Story of Billy and Hale)

The Twelfth of Never (Blind Faith 3.5)

Twelve Days of Christmas (Sixty Five Hours Christmas)

Best of Both Worlds

TRANSLATED TITLES:

ITALIAN

Fiducia Cieca (Blind Faith)

Attraverso Questi Occhi (Through These Eyes)

Preso alla Sprovvista (Blindside)

Il giorno del Mai (Blind Faith 3.5)

Cuore di Terra Rossa Serie (Red Dirt Heart Series)

Natale di terra rossa (Red dirt Christmas)

Intervento di Retrofit (Elements of Retrofit)

A Chiare Linee (Clarity of Lines)

Senso D'appartenenza (Sense of Place)

Spencer Cohen Serie (including Yanni's Story)

Punto di non Ritorno (Point of No Return)

Punto di Rottura (Breaking Point)
Punto di Partenza (Starting Point)
Imago (Imago)
Imagines
Il desiderio di un soldato (A Soldier's Wish)
Scambiato (Switched)
Tallowwood
The Hate You Drink
Ho trovato te (Finders Keepers)
Cuori d'argilla (Throwing Hearts)
Galassie e Oceani (Galaxies and Oceans)
Il peso di tut (The Weight of it All)
Pieces of You - Missing Pieces 1
Pieces of Me - Missing Pieces 2
Pieces of Us - Missing Pieces 3
Code Red

FRENCH

Confiance Aveugle (Blind Faith)
A travers ces yeux: Confiance Aveugle 2 (Through These Eyes)
Aveugle: Confiance Aveugle 3 (Blindside)
À Jamais (Blind Faith 3.5)
Cronin's Key Series

Au Coeur de Sutton Station (Red Dirt Heart)

Partir ou rester (Red Dirt Heart 2)

Faire Face (Red Dirt Heart 3)

Trouver sa Place (Red Dirt Heart 4)

Le Poids de Sentiments (The Weight of It All)

Un Noël à la sauce Henry (A Very Henry Christmas)

Une vie à Refaire (Switched)

Evolution (Evolved)

Galaxies & Océans

Qui Trouve, Garde (Finders Keepers)

Sens Dessus Dessous (Upside Down)

La Haine au Fond du Verre (The hate You Drink)

Tallowwood

Spencer Cohen Series

Thomas Elkin One

Lacuna

GERMAN

Flammende Erde (Red Dirt Heart)

Lodernde Erde (Red Dirt Heart 2)

Sengende Erde (Red Dirt Heart 3)

Ungezähmte Erde (Red Dirt Heart 4)

Vier Pfoten und ein bisschen Zufall (Finders Keepers)

Ein Kleines bisschen Versuchung (The Weight of It All)

Ein Kleines Bisschen Fur Immer (A Very Henry Christmas)

Weil Leibe uns immer Bliebt (Switched)

Drei Herzen eine Leibe (Three's Company)

Über uns die Sterne, zwischen uns die Liebe (Galaxies and Oceans)

Unnahbares Herz (Blind Faith 1)

Sehendes Herz (Blind Faith 2)

Hoffnungsvolles Herz (Blind Faith 3)

Verträumtes Herz (Blind Faith 3.5)

Thomas Elkin: Verlangen in neuem Design

Thomas Elkin: Leidenschaft in klaren

Thomas Elkin: Vertrauen in bester Lage

Traummann töpfern leicht gemacht (Throwing Hearts)

Sir

So Unendlich Viel Liebe (To the Moon and Back)

THAI

Sixty Five Hours (Thai translation)

Finders Keepers (Thai translation)

SPANISH

Sesenta y Cinco Horas (Sixty Five Hours)

Los Doce Días de Navidad

Código Rojo (Code Red)

Código Azul (Code Blue)

Queridísimo Milton James

Queridísimo Malachi Keogh

El Peso de Todo (The Weight of it All)

Tres Muérdagos en Raya: Serie Navidad en Hartbridge

Lista De Deseos Navideños: Serie Navidad en Hartbridge

Feliz Navidad Cupido: Serie Navidad en Hartbridge

Spencer Cohen Libro Uno

Spencer Cohen Libro Dos

Spencer Cohen Libro Tres

Davo

Hasta la Luna y de Vuelta

Venciendo A La Lluvia

En la Tempestad

El Toque del Rayo

Corazón De Tierra Roja

Corazón De Tierra Roja 2

Corazón De Tierra Roja 3

Corazón De Tierra Roja 4

ECB (Enemigos con Beneficios)

Floral

CHINESE

Blind Faith

Bossy

JAPANESE

Bossy

To the Moon and Back

PORTUGUESE

Sessenta e Cinco Horas

Printed in Dunstable, United Kingdom